INK STAINS

A DARK FICTION LITERARY ANTHOLOGY

Volume 2

Edited by
N. Apythia Morges

Dark Alley Press

INK STAINS ANTHOLOGY
Volume 2

ISBN 13: 978-1-946050-00-7

© 2016 by Dark Alley Press
Individual stories copyright by authors
"A Lonely Night" © 2016 by Brian Becker
"How the Other Half Lives" © 2016 by Melanie Marshall
"The Casual Absorbing of Melanie Woefler" © 2016 by Douglas Andrew Smith
"Ozzy Tate's Toe" © 2016 byDaniel Henshaw
"One for Sorrow" © 2016 by J.D. Kotzman
"Yellow Pill" © 2016 by I. K. Paterson-Harkness
"Spouse Swap" © 2016 by Cooper O'Connor

Dark Alley Press
http://www.darkalleypress.com

An imprint of Vagabondage Press LLC
PO Box 3563
Apollo Beach, Florida 33572
http://www.vagabondagepress.com

First edition printed in the United States of America and the United Kingdom, September 2016

10 9 8 7 6 5 4 3 2 1

Front cover art by Olexandr. Cover designed by Maggie Ward.

INK STAINS

A DARK FICTION LITERARY ANTHOLOGY

TABLE OF CONTENTS

A LONELY NIGHT

Brian Becker

The night sky spread out like a tent over the countryside. There were no clouds to block the light of the moon and the stars glimmering on the tall cornhusks. Far out into the cornfield, an aging but well-kept farmhouse sat next to a series of elongated buildings whose gleaming metal rooftops aggressively interrupted the picturesque rural backdrop. Bill Dubenmeyer trudged out of the barn to his house and up the stairs leading to his back door. He paused at the top while he took the last drag of his Winston full-flavor cigarette and turned to look across his yard and the cornfield beyond, sitting peacefully under the sky. Bill enjoyed the stars shining brightly in the night sky that you can only find far from the lights of the city. Only last weekend, Bill had visited his daughter in Des Moines, where she attended college, and noticed there were no stars to be seen. Being in the city made Bill feel on edge and closed off. But, out in the country on his farm with no one else for miles around, he felt at ease.

Exhaling the smoke out into the crisp night air and watching it drift up into the sky had a calming effect on Bill. At last he turned and opened the door to his back porch. Once inside, he used his bootjack to pull off his work boots for the day then turned and walked into the kitchen. After washing his hands, Bill pulled some leftover pork steak and potatoes from the fridge and put them in the microwave. Eating leftovers did not bother Bill, even after being treated to home-cooked meals made fresh every night during twenty-two years of marriage. For a few months after his wife, Sherry, ran away with her boyfriend, Bill's family and friends in the surrounding area brought him plates of food for dinner. Over time, these came less and less frequently, and in the end, he learned to cook for himself. Bill didn't mind this and enjoyed the peace and quiet he now had in the evenings. As far as loneliness was concerned, Bill was content, and for him, time seemed to drift by in a slow haze. He still had Jackson, his five-year-old black lab by his side at all times. Bill felt an attachment to Jackson, and they depended on one another for survival, even if in different ways.

As time went by, Bill's friends and neighbors saw less of him. He kept to himself, only venturing into town to pick up food and supplies for the farm. During the harvest season, some of the townsmen would work for Bill to help bring in his crop, but even during these times, Bill went about his work in a quiet, no-nonsense manner. Most people who knew Bill knew he had never been the outgoing type, but now that Sherry had left him, he had all but disappeared. When Sherry left, their old friends tried to convince Bill to go to the bar or county fair, but after numerous failed attempts, Bill stopped receiving invitations.

After finishing his meal and washing the dishes, Bill sat down in his recliner with a glass of bourbon on ice. He lit a cigarette and took a drink, closing his eyes as he swallowed it, feeling his throat warm as the bourbon slid down. He took a puff of his cigarette and was about to exhale when there was a loud knock at his door. Bill paused for a moment, then breathed out a thin cloud of smoke. He took another drink of his bourbon, sat the glass down, and stood up. He rolled the cigarette in his calloused fingers and took another long drag. He reluctantly put it out in the crystal ashtray Sherry had given him for their fifth anniversary. He always thought that the crystal seemed out of place in the old farmhouse but never had the heart to replace it.

Bill walked back into the kitchen. He paused before entering the hallway to the back door. His Winchester 30-30 rifle was leaning in the corner of the kitchen against the wall. He had a strong urge to grab the gun and carry it to the door with him. He wasn't sure why, but something made him anxious as he waited, listening again for this unusual late-night knock. Another knock came, louder this time, more urgent. Even after the second knock, he stood in the kitchen for another moment before entering the hallway and walking to the door empty-handed. As he reached the door, he switched on the porch light and saw two men standing on his back steps. The man closest to the door appeared to be in his fifties with a well-kept beard. He was dressed in old jeans, muddy boots, and a dark blue sweatshirt that looked to Bill as if it had seen better days. The man behind him was much shorter and younger, but wore similar clothes. He had a slight mustache that Bill guessed had taken quite a while for the young man to grow.

When Bill opened the door, the bearded man greeted him with a smile and introduced himself and his son. He explained that they were lost. They were looking for their cousin's house but must have missed the turn somewhere along the miles of twisting gravel roads. They ran out of gas and walked to the nearest house—Bill's. After hearing the man's explanation, Bill did not reply for a moment; he observed the two men in front of him. The older man looked expectantly at Bill. The younger man had his hands in his pockets and looked embarrassed. The older of the two men finally broke the silence and asked Bill if they could buy a can of gas from his farm supply.

"Who did you say your cousin was?" Bill questioned.

"I didn't. But her name is Laura Welbert," replied the bearded man.

"I don't know a Laura Welbert," Bill said.

"I'm sure you don't know her, and as I said we're lost; you see we're from Chicago and have never been to my cousins house." Bill stared back at the man but did not respond. "Look buddy, we've never been out here to see my cousin." Bill could see the man was beginning to get anxious. "We have directions." The man dug into his pocket for a moment then produced a handwritten note and excitedly held it up to Bill as if he had proven a point. "We didn't realize until we looked at our directions again after running out of gas that we had taken a wrong turn. We're still at least 100 miles from my cousin's house," the bearded man explained.

"I see," Bill replied, "and you have a gas can?"

"Yes," the man replied. After another uncomfortable silence, Bill could see the man was becoming irritated. "So, if you would just let us have some of your gas, we can be on our way and out of your hair...we can give you some money if you want."

Bill hesitated for a moment before replying "Okay, I suppose that wouldn't be a problem. Give me just a second while I put on my boots and grab my coat."

"Thank you," the bearded man said.

Bill closed the door and grabbed his coat. He thought for a moment and then put his hunting knife in the pocket. He was a little uneasy about walking out to the fuel tank in the dark with these two men, but with the knife in his pocket. he felt some reassurance.

He pulled his boots on, opened the door, and walked off his porch with Jackson where the two men waited. The younger man reached down to pet Jackson, but the dog began to growl.

Chuckling, Bill said, "Jackson isn't always real friendly to strangers. Sorry about that." Then continuing, "Follow me. The tank is out by the shed."

The men followed, and the bearded man asked, "So do you have any family here with you?"

"Nope, all by myself now. Just have the one daughter, but she's away at school in Des Moines."

"You must get lonely out here all by yourself," the bearded man said.

"Actually, I don't mind it at all. Jackson gives me all the company I need, and I enjoy the peace and quiet."

When they reached the fuel tank, Bill took the can from the son, switched on the pump, and bent over, putting the nozzle in the can and turning it on. As he did, he heard a click, which he recognized as the sound of the hammer being pulled back on a handgun. He slowly turned around and saw the bearded man looking down at him behind the barrel of a shiny silver pistol aimed straight at his face.

Bill calmly stood up and said, "So I guess it's safe to assume that you don't need any gas."

"That's right," the bearded man said. "Actually, we need to use something else that you have here on your farm..."—he paused—"I understand you have a large number of hogs you raise here, is that correct?"

"Yes," Bill said.

"Well we would like to feed them a late night meal we brought with us. Everything is ready; you just need to take us into your largest hog house and help us feed them. If you do that, then we will just drive off and leave you when we are done. But, if you give us any trouble or if you go call your sheriff and let him know that we've been here, then I'm afraid we would have to prepare another meal for your hogs. Do you understand?"

"I do."

"Just to make sure we are clear." The bearded man stepped closer, the gun now only inches from Bill's face. "If I hear of any small-time county sheriff looking for me or my boy, then we will be making a trip down to Des Moines, pick up your little girl, and bring her back here to cut up for your hogs along with you."

Bill felt anger begin to swell up inside him. The anger surpassed even what he had felt when Sherry had left him. He wanted to hurt this man for threatening his daughter, but his knife was no match for the man's gun. Bill had lost his wife, and now these men were threatening to take away his daughter. His stomach felt hollow, and his hand had a slight tremor. After a few breaths, Bill calmed himself, nodded his head, and said, "Okay, where is your food?"

"It's in the back of our truck just up the road," the man said, before turning to his son. "Go get the truck and drive it up here."

The younger man turned and began jogging down the drive, along the gravel road. The men stood in silence while they waited. Bill heard the door of the truck open and shut. The truck started. He heard it approach and soon saw the headlights turn up his drive.

Bill turned and began walking along the dirt road through his hog houses, motioning for them to follow. He continued walking all of the way to the back building then stopped and pointed toward the door. The young man stopped the truck and shut it off.

"Get back here and help us carry this in," the bearded man ordered Bill.

Bill walked around the back of the truck. The younger man opened the tailgate and untied the tarp covering the back, exposing several large plastic tubs with industrial grade garbage bags tied off in each of them. The younger man grabbed the first one, grunting as he lifted it off the back. Bill grabbed the next one, lifting it with ease, and carried it over to the door of the hog house. He sat down the tub before reaching into his jeans and pulling out his keys. Bill's fingers went straight to the key he wanted, and he inserted it into the lock, opening the door. He picked up his tub and walked in. He carried it to the middle of the hog house, through the familiar, narrow, dark walkways. The air was filled with the smell that can only be found where hundreds of animals are kept in a confined area with waste spread about their feet. The smell would be stifling to most, but it did not bother Bill as he made his way through the building. He could hear the young man struggling behind him with both the smell and the weight of the tub which he carried. Bill smiled to himself and thought, *at least he was telling the truth about being from the city. This kid has never worked a day in his life.*

Accompanying the smell was the constant squealing of the pigs and the loud banging of metal as the pigs moved against their pens. The building, which appeared massive from the outside, felt much smaller and claustrophobic once inside.

The dim lighting throughout the building created shadows that danced violently with the shifting pens. In the center of the building, they came to a dirt floor opening with room for at least a dozen hogs to roam about. In the middle, the lights were unobstructed and their intense light filled the area.

"We can feed them here," Bill said.

"Okay, let's go get the other two tubs," the bearded man replied.

Bill and the younger man carried the remaining two tubs into the center holding area.

"We can dump out these bags and then let the hogs into the holding pen," Bill said.

The bearded man nodded, and Bill grabbed the first bag and dumped it out onto the center of the dirt floor. He wasn't surprised when the rotten red chunks fell out onto the floor. He saw blood, flesh, pieces of bone, and hair all chopped and mixed together. The sight and smell didn't bother him; he butchered his own pigs, so he was used to the bloody mess. But, these weren't butchered pigs he was dumping out of the trash bags; this, Bill knew, had once been two living, breathing people. The bearded man continued to hold the gun as Bill dumped out the last of the bags.

Bill turned back to look at the men and saw the younger man was bothered much more than Bill or the man with the gun.

"I'm going to step outside for a little bit," said the younger man, then turned and walked back the way he came. Bill watched him leave for a moment then shrugged and climbed outside the pen. He opened the walkway for the pigs to move into the center, then climbed on top of the pens and began raising the individual gates allowing the pigs to file down the hallway and into the holding area. They began eating as soon as they reached the remains in the middle.

The bearded man watched the hogs begin to eat, devouring their food as fast as they could get it into their mouths. After a moment, he decided it was time to kill the farmer and get rid of him too. He looked down the rows where he had just been opening the gates but didn't see him. He spun around, looking behind him and to either side but saw nothing.

The excited pigs were squealing and grunting, sending echoes that bounced off the metal walls. The sounds filled the bearded man's head, and he began to move in the direction he had last seen the farmer. He reached the individual holding pens but could not see the man. Then he heard a noise moving toward him and started to turn but was too late. He felt cold metal slide into the middle of his back. Coolness rushed through his body, and his vision became cloudy as he fell limp and slumped to the floor. He felt the knife pulled out of his back, and the gun he had dropped was picked up and put into the farmer's pocket.

Outside the building, the young man took another puff from his cigarette before putting it out on the metal building then stuffing the butt into his pocket. He opened the door and was immediately hit with the loud squealing and metal banging; it was as if the whole building had come alive. The lights seemed dimmer now and flickered as he walked up the row to the middle. Halfway down the row, it turned in a different direction than he remembered. It was as if the metal gates had been moved to form a new path.

He stood staring down the walkway looking for the other men. His hand began to shake, and he clinched his fist to regain his composure. After a moment, he gathered himself and began to move down the new row. He surveyed the building around him as the path wound left and right through the holding pens. The row came to an end at the holding area in the middle. He counted at least a dozen hogs now, and while the ground was still covered in blood, all of the chunks of flesh and bone were gone. The hogs were gathered on the other side fighting and pushing one another trying to get at something.

One of the large pigs was pushed aside for a moment, and the young man saw the muddy boot of the bearded man sticking out from the pile. The pigs' snouts were covered in blood as they squealed in excitement trying to get to the meat.

"Oh my god," he whispered to himself.

Then he saw movement to his right, and the farmer swung a heavy metal pipe into the young man's chest. He heard a crack as his ribs broke, and he was slammed backward against the metal. He gasped desperately for breath as his broken bones pushed against his lungs. The farmer climbed over the railing and stood for a moment staring down at the boy. The farmer's face was expressionless, and his eyes were cold and faraway.

"Please," the boy begged.

Then without hesitating, the farmer raised the pipe and swung it down on the young man's knees. He screamed in pain, writhing on the ground trying to get distance between him and the farmer. He pushed himself backward until he came up against the metal gate between him and the hogs. The farmer didn't follow him; instead he took a step back. He slid another gate between himself and the boy. Then reaching up, he pulled down a lever above his head, and as he did, it raised the gate behind the boy, opening him up to the hogs. Once it was open there was no time to escape, the animals were ready.

✕✕✕

Bill turned and walked down the rows and out of the building, listening to the squealing behind him. It was possible there were screams mixed in, but if there were, they soon faded away. Bill reached the door and locked it behind him as he lit another cigarette. Jackson trotted over to him, and Bill reached down and tenderly scratched his neck. Then looking up into the wide night sky, Bill breathed out smoke and smiled to himself.

After getting back to his house, he poured himself another bourbon and sat down in his chair. He knew these men would be missed, but the police wouldn't be contacted. Someone else would come looking for them, and when they did, he would be here waiting. He sat in his chair, sipping bourbon, thinking about the two men who had knocked on his door tonight. They had now gone missing just like his wife and her boyfriend. Most people assumed they had run away together, but Bill knew better. Smiling again, he took another drink and waited for another knock at the door.

)(O)(O)( )(O)(O)( )(O)(O)( )(

ABOUT THE AUTHOR

Brian Becker resides in Kansas City, Missouri, with his wife, Amy, son, James, and dog, Jackson. He enjoys conjuring stories of fiction that explore the lengths to which people will endeavor when faced with difficult and often times malevolent circumstances. When he isn't writing or changing diapers, he is probably spending his time planning his next vacation.

How the Other Half Lives

Melanie Marshall

The night swoops. It being December, I should have been prepared. My hands are barely able to grasp the Maglite torch in the chill. A line of light bounces off the shifting water. I've been following the river since dawn. Now it's only a stream, and I'm no closer to my destination, I fear. I shift the weight of the rucksack. The ache in my shoulders and back impedes my progress, nearly thirty years old and does my body know it. This is just about the first strenuous exercise I've done in months, unless you count running for the tube most mornings, or that night with Jonno's ex, Marie. The less I think about that whole fucking mess, the better.

I've read about the fog, how it descends on the moor and disorientates men to the point of death. Not that I'm scared yet. I should have reached Ashgard in time for dinner; the log fire and six real ales are calling me now from The Highwayman Inn where I've booked a room.

Lonesome orienteering seemed such a freeing idea. I'd use up all my five remaining days of leave from Clifford & Dyer before Christmas, offsetting all of those endless city days. "Leave," as if we were some kind of goddamn soldiers. Instead, we're advertising execs, splattering consumers' blood across billboards and websites.

Spears jut from the gloom. Only the branches of a leafless tree... Hills, roads, and rivers disappear down the creases of the ordnance survey map; everything is a damp crevice that I'm straining to see. My lenses are playing up, blurred and scratching on the jelly of my eyes. Sleep would be good. I continue on in the same direction, brand new hiking boots dead weights. The stream veers off now. I'm on my own. My body is a compass needle, I tell myself, bobbing and adjusting and finding the right path. Yes, yes, screw you, Dyer. I can do this. I am able to function without my iPhone-shaped life support.

Ten minutes forward. Can't tell if the mist is from my contact lenses or it's meteorological. My feet find tufty grass, in among the scree. It's not quite cold enough for frost. If Marie could see me now. She'd probably still ignore me, turning to her iMac screen with a shake of her perfect, perfect mane. The night is crouching, still, anticipating me. Ahead, something, Gorgon-headed. Seriously, no. It can't be. The same bloody tree from before, arching over the stream and glittering in its death dance. From all sides, there is bleating, then barking, sheep, sure, but…a black dog, a Labrador, comes vaulting through the mist. Now its paws pound on my chest, and I stumble back.

"Nero! Stop that. Heel!" The creature duly whines and finds his master's wellied feet. The rest of the man appears in my torchlight beam like a falcon, silvery hair, strong nose.

"Hello there," he says, eyebrows raised. "Are you lost?"

I croak affirmative, lost and hungry and cold.

"Christ," he says, "people have perished out here on milder nights than this. Come, my place isn't far."

I don't resist. We walk together, exchange a few words; his name is Rufus. I estimate he's in his late fifties. He seems unwary of me, so I'm unwary of him. I focus on the sound of his wax jacket rumpling as he moves, Nero's panting, until I can barely feel my toes anymore, and then I can smell wood smoke at last. There are wrought iron gates and a drive, illuminated with lanterns. The gates need a lick of paint; several of the lanterns' bulbs are gone. There are weeds in the gravel.

We pass an old Jag on bricks, an MG poking from a tarpaulin

"My other cars are in there," he gestures to a stable block.

Of course, he's a target audience for premium vintage cars, I note, and then as the drive slopes down, off the moor, the house rises up. A stone farmhouse, several windows lit. The stone above the door reads 1678 in ecclesiastical font. Rufus ushers me inside first, and I'm a small boy who's said yes to a stranger.

"I shouldn't stay long," I say.

"Have a drink at least, Steven," he says.

"Could I please use your phone, first?"

"We don't have one, I'm afraid, nor one of those mobile ones, strange as that might sound to you," he replies.

You have no idea, mate.

"Where were you heading?" he asks. I tell him.

"You've strayed off course a heck of a long way," he says, in his vaguely school masterish manner. "Stay the night."

"No, I couldn't." I'm not sure whether it's caution or politeness is making me resist.

"Don't be ridiculous. There's masses of room. And we can't drive you anywhere as we've all been drinking."

I shake my head but follow him all the same. The wood-paneled hall leads into a dimly lit and very large, kitchen. Nutmeg and savory aromas hang in the warmth. An incredibly attractive woman, wearing an earthy knitted dress with her dark hair in a topknot is standing at the Rayburn. This literally looks like an ad we recently placed in *Country Life*, although with a lot more dust. An open newspaper and a scraped-clean bowl with fork rest on the banquet table. There are lots of used wineglasses: I count seven, and several empty bottles, too.

"Hello," she says, in a mistrustful tone.

Rufus explains what happened, and the woman frowns.

"This is Olivia," he says, not saying "My wife" or "partner," so I'm none the wiser. Neither of them wear wedding rings. He squeezes her waist and smiles. I choose to sit down on the long bench by the table, before I fall down.

"There's leftover stew," Olivia says. I want to politely refuse, but my stomach thinks otherwise. Soon, I'm shoveling in melting meat with dumplings the size of fists, rinsed down with what's left of the red wine. The dog is curled up by the Rayburn now, and I notice shelves and shelves above full of jars of lentils, herbs, and dried mushrooms and foodstuffs I can't even identify, right up to the beams in the ceiling.

"Lovely place you've got here." They are silent. "I thought there was nothing out here on the moor," I continue, "but I suppose some wealthy merchant with horses would have built his country retirement gaff back in the day."

Rufus and Olivia exchange glances. I wonder if it means they're regretting finding me. Most people regret finding me.

"The house has been in my family for quite some years," Rufus says. "The upkeep's not easy, but then we're mainly self-sufficient. The mutton you're eating was one of our sheep."

I nod, awkward.

"When you're done, I'll give you *le grand* tour," he says.

Olivia purses her mouth, just perceptible in the murky kitchen. There is the threat of wrinkles on her brow, but I wouldn't like to guess her age. Slightly his junior, maybe. I excuse myself to use their loo, another of the many doorways off the hall. As I piss, I hear voices bickering through the wall. She's blistering with rage, but I can't make out the words. His voice is low and level.

Back out in the corridor, the whine of accordion music is oozing from upstairs. I take off my coat and fleece, rub my aching eyes. One room I pass is lit by coals seething in the fireplace. I peer around and see a young woman lounging on a Chesterfield, draped in tartan blankets. She doesn't look up. Rufus appears from the kitchen, pink in his previously pale cheeks.

The tour takes us to the top of the house first. There are tons of paintings on the walls, portraits, and modern, bright stuff too. I don't know much about art, only Getty Images. We enter four bedrooms. The first is his, he tells me. A four-poster governs the space. The next two rooms, interlinked by a bathroom, are decorated in burgundies and forest greens, with carved oak beds. The second is empty, but the third room contains two girls, no older than seventeen, I forget their names as quickly as I hear them, although they're something Shakespearean or mythical as far as I can tell. They're listening to records, sitting on the floor, reading from leather-bound tomes. "Hi darling," they say to Rufus as we pass, which sets off a Catherine Wheel of questions in my head, none of which I dare ask. A grandfather clock strikes in the corner, and I jump.

The last room has two girls playing a game of Scrabble on the bed. I'm struck by the ennui in these scenes, set-pieces in an endless loop, like big cats at the zoo. They look no older than twenty, one red-head, a small belly protruding over the top of her Indian trousers, and the other a brunette with vaguely buck-teeth that do nothing to detract from her beauty. The brunette gets up and begins dancing to the continental tune emanating from a record player. She's drinking straight from a wine bottle. She swishes over in her velvet dress and kimono, a combination that seems as though pulled from a posh dressing-up box.

She places an elegant hand in my palm. "Lavinia. Pleased to meet you."

"Are we going to light the bonfire soon?" she asks, huffy as a child, and places her mouth on Rufus'. He returns the unembarrassed kiss.

"Soon, darling, soon."

They make a handsome couple. I look away. The curtains aren't drawn. Beyond the leaded panes, interminable dark. All of a sudden, I wish I were wearing my fleece again. On our way back down the staircases, I must be staring at Rufus slack-jawed because he says, "What is it?"

"It's just…you live here, with all these women?"

"Yes, we cohabit." As though it was as commonplace as having a pet. "It's our midwinter celebration, as we jokingly call it," Rufus continues. "We're not pagans, but nature is good to us. There's so much alcohol to be imbibed, it's lucky that you arrived to share it with us."

"Sounds good to me." I think with a glimmer of guilt of my parents with their yearly glasses of Advocaat on Christmas Eve. Quicker than quick, he's poured me a whisky from the liquor cabinet.

"Girls!" he bellows through the house. Coats are dispensed from an understair cupboard, decadent furs and afghans—they could give the RSC costume department a run for their money. I turn to retrieve my own coat and come face to face with Olivia. My smile isn't returned, and I slope out to the back door after Rufus.

The girl from the living room, Tamara, I think, catches up with me. Violet-eyed like a young Elizabeth Taylor.

"So you're a waif and stray." The way she says it makes me prickle. "*Trust* Rufus to rescue someone on the moor. He's *such* a Mother

Teresa. Even gave the bloody dog a home when no one else wanted it."

"Don't worry, I'll be gone soon enough. Gotta get to my folks for Christmas anyway," I say. My dad had a heart attack in the summer, and I have yet to visit again. My guilt-levels are topped up, remembering him on the hospital gurney.

"Oh no, I wasn't saying that," she laughs. "Just that it's typical Rufus behavior. That's all."

Outdoors, I'm on my third whisky in half an hour, the bonfire has grown large and crackling, smoke and fog—burning paraffin. Swilling the wonderfully peaty liquid around my mouth, I try to remember the last time I've seen real fire. Maybe a Tandoori oven in Brick Lane. Tamara smells of wine. She links her arm in mine and shivers. I struggle to get women to like me in London; why should they like me any better here?

Rufus is booming "...this is very much like the winter solstice, but we do things our own way here, don't we?" And to the right of him, Olivia stands, her mouth hidden beneath a Fairisle scarf. Her eyes dance over the girls and me.

Lavinia and one of the others, the younger ones, whose name flees from me across the moor, are holding hands high above their heads, making weird shapes in the firelight. From this angle, it seems as though twigs and branches protrude from their bodies, and they are half-tree, half-girl. God, I am drunk.

"How are you over there, young man. Are you warm? Are you still alive?" Rufus guffaws, and his silvery hair gleams.

"When you're not wandering out in the wilderness, what do you do for a living?" the redhead asks, her beautifully angular face poking out from under a hood.

"Don't judge me, but I'm an ad exec." I realize how refreshing it is to actually be conversing with people who are not also ad execs, be it rivals or colleagues. Suck on that, Jonno and Marie. And here I am drinking some damn fine Scotch in the open air, not over-priced piss in a surgically lit bar.

The redhead frowns at my answer but doesn't elaborate.

"What about you?" I ask. There are eyes on me from all around the bonfire. Wrong question. Lavinia squeezes my arm. "Silly."

Olivia clears her throat. "Some of us paint, write, others work the land—every type of vegetable and fruit trees, cider. There are animals to look after...to slaughter..."

As if an incarnation of my embarrassment, a cat slinks along the side of the fire like a shadow. To accentuate nothing seeming real, tiny speckles drift from the sky over the flames. Snow.

Tamara huddles in closer. She suddenly lets out a tremendous "whoop" into the sky, which I can only assume is about the change in weather. Someone else yells, and Rufus laughs. "Freedom of expression, that's what we like." Cold wet fingers first of the top of my head and then my face.

Tamara jabs my side, her face swimming in front of me. "Your turn." My voice comes out as a pathetic little "yeah!" as though my voice has yet to break.

Rufus shouts over. I wonder if he can sing. He has that kind of baritone. "Come on now. Poor effort. You're alive, you're not lost anymore, that's something to be thankful for, is it not?" His coat is billowing into the dark.

"We have no neighbors; you can make as much noise as you like here," Olivia says, without turning to look at me.

So I really go for it, a howling bellow that ripples through the snow falling in front of me, swells out above their heads and into the firs beyond. What a daft game.

"That's better," Rufus says.

Tamara pats my arse, and I flinch forward a bit.

Olivia is ripping up paper, screwing it into balls, and lobbing it into the flames. I lean in to see it better. Maybe it's an electric bill or something similarly bourgeoisie. All of a sudden, the twisting lines and dots encased in a shiny cover comes into focus. It's my OS map.

"Hey, that's mine," I say. "*Was* mine."

She coolly stares. "It got damp and ripped, it would have been no good at all." She looks back to Rufus. "You can borrow ours if you need one."

The grievance flies from my mind…I don't know where the bottle appears from, angular glass with a solid brassy disc for a top. Mosstowie, Signatory Vintage, I make out in the flames, snaking S and a jutting V. Already the bottle is dusted in snowflakes.

"Thirty-year-old single malt," Rufus says, the side of his mouth rising. This is for savoring, a collector's item, not for getting wankered by a bonfire on.

But we drink and we drink. And the fire crackles and sputters. No moon watches over us. We are free to do as we please. I shake my head, laugh aloud. I am not one of them. But my blood thickens, and my heart fills up at the sight of these gorgeous folk, so far from the world.

"Do you have any vices?" Tamara whispers.

"None," I say, as I neck more from another bottle. Opposite, one of the other women hurls the empties into the flames. I hear the glass shatter, but I can't see it.

After I'm not sure how much more, some of the younger girls are still shouting noises into the night, Rufus and Olivia are locked in an embrace dancing together—the hard booze has obviously loosened her. Lavinia and the redhead, who I find is called Chloe, are sitting cross-legged on the snowy ground like children. They are both stroking Chloe's belly, smiling to each other in the dying glow.

Tamara sees me looking and gives a condescending nod. She leads me back to the house; all I see is her silk paisley skirt and wellies as we prop each other up along the path. We're shivering no more: the whisky has coated us.

We make it to a room on the second floor, lit with one faint lamp. Shedding my coat, I go to sit down in a leather armchair. There's an awful screech beneath me, and I leap up as a cat scarpers from the room. I fall over to the bed; the walls tilt and roll. I lay on my back, spread out on the throw across the bed. It feels like velvet. She's standing near, long fingers unbuttoning her blouse from the bottom, and there's crimson and navy underneath, straps falling down and lace slipping off. I don't get to see it, because the night swoops in again, and all I see and hear and taste is black.

XXX

The first thing I'm aware of is the cold—on my face, on my arms. Was last night all just a chill-induced mirage? Am I actually still out on the moor, in the snow? The tightening elastic band of a headache negates that theory. The curtains are still open; I suspect they were never closed. Harsh light streams into my eyes like a sophisticated form of torture. In my memory, a flash of Tamara's large nipples. I sit up with a start, erect in every sense. I am alone. Her fur cape hangs from the back of the chair like a taxidermist's prize. It adds to the curdling bile in my throat. I make for the bathroom, find I'm still fully clothed on standing. A mixture of disappointment and relief spills from my mouth into the toilet bowl.

Splashing water across the bristle on my face, the ghoul looking back from the mirror provokes me. *As if she would want you. As if you are fit for anything other than sloppy seconds like Marie.* Back along the landing, most doors are closed. The one that's ajar, the third room I saw yesterday, exposes not only bed sheets and empty bottles, but also a pair of hairy buttocks. The sleeping partner next to them is not Olivia. The grandfather clock tick-tocks in the corner.

The round window halfway down the stairs reveals something I hadn't remembered; the garden, complete with polytunnel and beanpoles, pigsty and stable roofs, and the moor all around are thick with snow. I find my rucksack at the foot of the stairs, a welcome hint. I pack the remainder of my belongings into it and head for the kitchen from where the smell of cooking drifts. Now my stomach's empty, I need to fill it again, quick. A pot gurgles on the stove.

"Porridge. Help yourself," Olivia says, barely looking away from the window. With daylight on her skin and no eye make-up, she is older, the wife I always imagined I'd have later in life. She rubs lotion into her hands, looks out at the white.

"It's like the world's telling us something, starting anew," she muses. I have no idea how to respond.

"I'll get going later, if you can set me on the right course" I say. "Please could I have that map?"

"Of course. First, you must eat."

I take the bowl of hot oats outside and stand in the snow.

XOXOX

Rufus finds me with my rucksack at my side, spoon in my mouth. Nero bounds off into the garden. Rufus seemingly disproves the fact that hangovers are worse the older you get, with his eyes full of light and his skin clear. Maybe it's lying with seventeen-year-olds that keeps him young.

"Olivia tells me you're off," he says. There's a pause. "We won't be able to move a vehicle through all this, and you won't find your way today. I'm telling you, worse than the dark—snow blindness."

I picture what awaits me, the pub, where I don't know anyone, then mum and dad's magnolia sitting room, then, after that, the office again.

"All right, but this lot better melt by Christmas Eve. No way I can stay." Words sink into the snow and are muffled. "Could be worse. We can cozy up with the Man U-Sunderland game. You a footie fan?"

"Ah, we don't have a television. Not really something we believe in."

"Like Santa Claus?" I immediately want to scoop that back into my mouth.

He sniffs. "Walk with me, Steven."

I gesture to the bowl in my hand.

"Leave it on the step for now."

I nod. The fear that he knows what happened, or nearly happened, with Tamara winds itself around my spine. Does she belong to him? Have I broken some kind of moorland etiquette?

We trudge through snow nothing else has touched, except for the odd bird. Nero stays at Rufus' side. He doesn't have a collar or a lead. Perhaps they don't believe in those, either.

We enter some woodland to the side of the house. Branches sag with the heaviness. "You can see from last night's fun that we don't live a normal existence. And it is good for us, for all of us. You're a bright man, good job in the city. I can see you understand."

Do I, hell.

"It's not often we receive visitors, especially not young men, and therefore you have caused quite a stir. But I'm so very glad we met." His tone is even.

Here it comes, the warning. But before it does, we've reached a clearing, and there at the edge of the field, russet against the bluish-white, four does and a stag. We watch in silence. I keep looking down at Nero in case he bolts, but he parks his bum in the snow and is quiet. One of the does hops aboard the back of another… "Are they…what are they doing?" I whisper.

"She's showing the stag that she's ready for him," he says with a smirk. "Lucky fellow, hey." Sure enough, when one doe climbs down, the stag gallops over and rears up to please.

"He's an old 'un," Rufus says. "See how broad he is across the rump and neck. He'll be replaced by one from another herd soon enough."

We continue watching; it seems like an age. I think of everything I do in the city and how hollow it all is. The trees absorb our silence. We creep back onto the woodland path. Mauve clouds threaten more snow. Out in front is an obelisk, tall and pale gray spike into the sky. It's the only structure as far as the eye can see.

"My great grandfather commissioned that. We remember everything he did for the family every time we see it. I will leave slightly less of a lasting mark," he pauses again. "I have brain cancer, and I'm dying, Steven."

I gawp.

"Until then, I am enjoying every day."

December 23rd, and no thaw. The room rolls amber as I swirl whisky around the cut crystal tumbler. It's long, long past midnight; these people do not believe in early nights. A fire spits in the grate. Sleep is in the foreground: the click-clunk of the record player needle next to me sounds hundreds of miles away. Today, I've been chopping logs. Since I'm more used to cropping images on Photoshop, every muscle in my back is strained. I am only just beginning to feel my fingers again.

Lavinia grasps Chloe's long locks and folds one strand over another into an intricate plait. Pampering seems to have been the theme of this evening. One of the younger girls, Mary, smooths a concoction of honey and yogurt onto her forehead. Tamara is sitting the furthest away from me, painting her toenails crimson. I look away in case she catches me staring, not at her bare ankles, but at the two stumps that round off her right foot. The sharp edge of the girls' existence is revealing itself—axes and beasts, chainsaws and vicious storms. Mine—vodka shots and deadlines, tube trains and rejections—is fading to a dull ache. Rufus appears, dragging a log basket that must be three times his weight. I leap up, "Want a hand with that?" He shakes his head. I've been searching for signs of it—the gnawing disease inside him, but all I see is smiles.

In an urge to expel some of those questions that have been multiplying in my head, I ask, "So, Tamara, how did you come to live here?" I ask.

I'm bored, granted, but no one's talking, so I may as well start something, chisel away these smiles a piece at a time

She laughs, pauses. "Do you know, I can barely remember."

"Drunk again, Tam-Tam?" says Mary.

Rufus doesn't chime in. He places a log on the fire, then curls himself around Tamara on the rug. She strokes his leg. Cool envy slides into me.

"You were probably in a bad way then?" I say.

Tamara shakes her head, lowers her brow, concentrating on the nail varnish brush. Over the hiss of the fire, I can almost hear her screaming. We haven't touched since the night of my arrival and have exchanged few niceties. Gone and done it again, haven't I? Got too close, too quick, and now it's all an awkward mess.

I move my metaphorical spotlight. "What about you, Lavinia?"

She doesn't miss a beat. "Well, I rolled here on a particularly fluffy nimbus cloud…"

They all giggle. For fuck's sake.

"A straight answer?"

Rufus lets out a breath.

Lavinia's mouth curls. "Okay, okay…the truth is, Rufus and Olivia were out gardening, planting trees, digging and digging the deep red earth with a spade, when they uncovered a shape…and there I was, perfectly formed, like Eve made from the clay,"

"Eve was supposedly made from Adam's rib, you fool," Olivia says, appearing in the doorway with a tea towel in her hand.

The room rings with laughter.

I register Rufus saying, "You're becoming quite the storyteller, Lavvy," but I've already swigged the whisky dregs, murmured, "fuck you all," and marched from the room.

Outside, the light from the window is in an orange strip across the snow. I peer in. Rufus kisses Olivia, while still wrapped around Tamara. Combined with the liquor coating my tongue, this makes me feel sick. My insides are heavy with dinner. I stand for while. Let them stew. I wish I smoked so that I could light up. Might keep me warm. I don't know how much time passes. The tall pines sway, the stars above immovable. In the breeze, I can almost hear the squeal of a pig fighting for life—whether it's imagined or remembered, I'm not sure. Were they slaughtering animals today while I was chopping wood? Nero pads out beside me and plonks himself down on the step. I could stay here, shaded from London's glare, and do indelicate things with wild creatures for the rest of my days. I shake my head. No. I need to get the hell out.

"The sky is never the same color at night." Rufus is close beside me all of a sudden, arm touching mine. I shuffle away slightly and make a *pffit* sound. I'm in no mood for his platitudes, whether he's dying or not.

"I didn't take the girls in, if that's what you think. They belong here, and it scares me to think of them alone when I'm gone," he says.

I shrug. "I thought they were strays. You like to collect things, people."

"*Strays?*" he grimaces. "You have quite the attitude to women, Steven, for such a young man."

Despair clasps my shoulders. "I really need to leave. Please. I need to borrow a car."

"You've had a bit to drink and…"

I stomp out through the snowy garden, rip the tarpaulin from the old Jag and the MG. Snow and debris scatters. There's a gaping hole in the bonnet of one, the other has no wheels. Of course.

"What about the others in the stables?" The aggression in my voice surprises me.

"They're just scraps. Projects I've been meaning to complete."

"Right."

I walk back over. He's in front of the window now. Olivia, Lavinia, Tamara, Mary, Chloe: all of them, dancing in the room behind him.

On the way back in, the holly wreath on the door catches on my T-shirted arm, draws blood. The laughter and dancing has finished; the girls have gone to their beds. A clock strikes five times; I had no idea it was that late. I head to the back room where I slept last night in an armchair to avoid the possibility of sex. It seems absurd now. My rucksack and coat aren't there. I go to the understairs cupboard. Not there. A map, at least, would be good. On the bookshelves, rows and row of classics but nothing so utilitarian. Shelves in the hallway hold binoculars, drawing pins, brooches, and a plastic-wrapped tampon but no map. I grab a torch hanging from a hook. I remember some papers and bits shoved into a rack in the kitchen. There's a bill addressed to Mr. R. A. Hayward-Young, a Countryside Alliance newsletter, some junk. The electoral register form. These people *vote*. I scan down expecting only to see Rufus' name, but there are several "residents over the age of eighteen" listed. Ms. T Hayward-Young, Ms. L Hayward-Young, Ms. C Hayward-Young…My stomach turns over itself.

The oak bureau in the back room. I sprint there, making as little noise as possible on the floorboards. The bureau's locked, but the tiny key is in the lock, pretty futile. The paperwork inside is sparse, especially for people who don't own a PC. Everything is in separate cream envelopes, thick textured paper with sharp creases. Apart from a map, I don't know what I'm even looking for here. Verification, perhaps. In the third envelope rests Rufus' will. I get the gist that everything is left to Olivia. In another, a bundle of birth certificates. Mother's forenames: Olivia Jean, Father's forenames: Rufus Alexander, one for each of the girls. Every muscle in my body contracts. I'm cold to the core.

At the top of the stairs, Rufus and Chloe embrace; her red hair tumbles over his shoulder. He peels away to reveal the full extent of her belly, naked and strained where her pajama top has rolled up—her navel convex. Smiles buckle their jaws. I grab a sheepskin coat from the cupboard and run, torch in my other hand. Reaching the kitchen, I nearly slam into Tamara. She is in silk pajamas, drinking from a mug.

"In a hurry?" she says, indigo eyes wide.

"I know…"

She frowns. "What?"

"I know… what you are."

"What are you talking about, Steven?" She places a hand on my shoulder. I don't move away.

The heat of her breath on my face chills my insides all the more. "Come with me. You don't have to live like this," I say.

"Don't be daft. Stay. You don't have to go anywhere."

Of course, it's all she knows. She wouldn't last a day in my world. Just imagine her negotiating the tube or as working as a secretary in an office. I look down at the floor. She's not wearing socks or slippers. The red varnish on her deformed foot looks almost painful.

"Steven?" I hear Rufus' voice behind me.

I leave then, move from hot air to cold. Fast footprints in the snow is all that will be left of me…—"Wait!" he yells—…except my rucksack that someone must have hidden. I rack my brain as I run: Do any of my belongings have an address on? Can they trace me? I don't think so. It's not like I'm going to the police with their sick little secret anyway, the consequences, the explanations, so much more that I could handle. I've been sprinting for a couple of minutes, and breaths come jerking from my lungs, my calf muscles taut. The sky's opened again. Fat lumps of icy wet fall in my eyes. Branches jut like bone. If only I had a clue where I was heading. Away from them, that's all I know. The torch is less than useful when the whole lot is so white and gray. In exposed patches, the snow's turned to slush. I run while there is still force in me to run. I turn where there's a turn in the path. My feet slide under me, I flail for branches, anything, to keep me upright, but I'm down on my arse, and my throat is stinging and my hands ache. Adrenaline gives way to throbbing pain. What an idiotic decision. I'll perish out here for sure. Maybe it's better than the alternative—looking after that coven when Rufus abandons the mortal coil. Bruised and sore, I scrabble to my feet, limp on.

It hasn't been long enough since I left the house, but the path seems to have bypassed the acres and acres of moor and forest I was anticipating. Ahead, a road, with street lamps, with houses, empty save for a couple of snowmen in front gardens. I brush snow from my eyes. I spew a half-laugh, half-strangled cry. The sign says *Welcome to Ashgard. Thank you for driving carefully.* Along the road hangs the illuminated sign of The Highwayman Inn. Turning back, less than a mile away, I can still make out the sketchy outline of their house in the white dawn.

✕◊✕✕ ✕◊✕✕ ✕◊✕✕ ✕

ABOUT THE AUTHOR

Melanie Marshall is a freelance editor and writer from Somerset, England. Her stories have been published by *The Moth, The Ghastling, Momaya Press, Prole Books,* and her yet unpublished novel was long listed for the Mslexia Prize 2013. She completed the prestigious MA in creative writing at the University of East Anglia. She enjoys dark fiction by Angela Carter, M.R. James, H.P. Lovecraft, Jeremy Dyson, Neil Gaiman, and Robert Aickman.

THE CASUAL ABSORBING OF MELANIE WOEFLER

Douglas Andrew Smith

Melanie Woefler was standing in front of an end cap at the Wal-Mart gaping at a display of cranberry-flavored Sierra Mist. $3.99 for a twelve-pack. A steal! Dang it though, she'd already stocked up on pop at the Save-A-Lot. Twelve would put her over her $50 budget, and she wasn't about to surrender the hemorrhoid cream, the Adele CD, or the XXXL cotton panties. Nothing in her drawer was going to survive another washing. She sighed and checked out with what she had already loaded into the cart. It totaled $47.83.

The shopping change always went toward scratch tickets at the Speedy-Mart, except for last week. The Powerball jackpot was pushing three-hundred-million so she grabbed one of those instead. Before picking up a Treasure Chest or a Big Money, she routed through her worn denim purse for the receipt. She found it crumpled at the bottom with some Vaseline lip balm and burnt red hair pasted to it. After scanning it under the automated device, she bounced her jaw off the floor a few times. She didn't hit the jackpot, but she matched five numbers: 6, 12, 23, 25, and 36. The only number she missed was the Powerball number: 21. The ticket was worth $1,595,867.32.

Melanie was a rich woman. But that didn't change the fact that her only way home was the bus. She couldn't wait to tell her mother that the universe had finally stopped kicking the Woeflers in the gut. But she never got to. At home, she found her mother dead in the faded blue recliner that used to be her dad's. Rigor mortis had already set in. A commercial for Depends adult under-garments was blaring across the room (Mom was a little hard of hearing). Melanie hit the off button on the remote control and then pried the device away from her mother's cold gray fingers.

Melanie never felt guilty about not being sad at that moment. She stood there in the midst of the rare silence and let the feeling of freedom wash over her. She felt ethereal for awhile, until suddenly she had to go poop. When she was recollected inside of her own head, she discovered that she wasn't thinking about her mother at all. She was thinking about something that she recently spotted for sale in one of the neighbor's driveways, something that she could now go and buy if she wanted to.

First Melanie had to get the money. No, first she had to deal with the dead body. It was already starting to smell worse than usual. No, first she had to do something about her mother's final resting pose. She closed her eyes, and her life flickered in front of her, and it looked like a spliced reel of game shows, soap operas, news events, and hockey games. When she opened her eyes, she saw everything through a new lens. It was surreal and hopeful, as though she'd sprouted wings and could soar above the person she used to be. Melanie wasn't strong enough to move Mom. She had to kill the television instead.

In a small barn just outside the back door, there remained a few tools that hadn't been hocked or stolen since Dad drowned in a grain silo more than a decade ago. One of those tools was a ten-pound sledgehammer. The sledgehammer held some special significance for Melanie, and it was the reason that she had made a point of hanging on to it all these years. About a week before Dad died, he busted the handle on the sledge while splitting a cord of hickory with steel wedges. Dad made a big thing out of showing Melanie how to replace the wooden handle, sliding it up through the hole in the tool's head, and then setting it into place using two perpendicular wedges. Shopping for the new handle and getting it installed took all afternoon, and no more wood ever wound up getting split with it after. Dad died before he could finish cutting the pile. The bigger rounds of the hickory had been sitting there, rotting, ever since.

It seems to weigh a lot more than ten pounds, thought Melanie as she hauled the tool inside. She kept her left hand close to the head so she had good control. Her right hand she kept about two thirds of the way down the handle. Melanie placed the head of the tool close to the television screen and practiced her stroke with her fish-eye reflection. Then she took one long back swing and with all she had, she buried the business end of the sledge hammer inside the guts of the television. Glass shattered and poured down within the innards of the set, and Melanie stood there kind of star struck, observing the unit's intestines. How could something so inanimate have held so much power over them? The sight filled her with a big, weird respect for the thing. She also respected herself for having the fortitude to destroy it. The remainder of her life was going to take place outside of that house. She was standing on rock bottom, and it was time to swim up. She had money. She had time. And she had no one but herself to be responsible for.

Half an hour later, two young EMTs showed up to collect the body of the mother. One of them was a short, stout, Mexican kid who went by Lupé. He seemed like he was just out of training and rather green as a field agent. The man in charge was called Glen. He was reassuringly tall and muscular (it was going to take some brawn to get Mom out of the chair), with olive skin, a push broom mustache, and a very practical short haircut that was lacking in any style. Both Lupé and Glen seemed to be having a harder time dealing with the violence that had been inflicted on the television than they were with the dead woman.

"Did she break that TV before she died?" asked Glen. His tone was unsettled, as though he had seen a lot of disturbing things before but never this.

"I broke it," said Melanie with a clear and resolute confidence that wasn't available to her earlier in the day.

"What on earth for?" said Lupé.

"Sick of that thing. It killed my mother."

"Televisions don't kill people," said Glen. "Sure, people could probably afford to watch a little less. Especially the reality crap." Which happened to be Melanie's favorite.

"If you didn't want it anymore, you could have just put it on the curb. I bet a neighbor would have picked it up," said Lupé.

"I wasn't trying to break a television set. I was venting anger at something that has been stealing time from me for as long as I can remember anything at all. That stupid thing killed my mother. I wanted it dead. Now, please just do your job. I'll get someone else to come over and deal with the set."

It wasn't easy for the two men to get the big woman onto the gurney. On their way out the door, Melanie heard Lupé complaining about pain in his lower lumbar.

After they left, Melanie took a quick walk up Maple Street, left on C, and then right on Doss. She had spied something for sale over there and wanted to make sure that it was still available. It was.

Melanie used the money to hire a lawyer to streamline the process of having Mom's estate put in her name so she could sell everything. The "for sale" sign was planted in the front lawn on the same day Mom's body was cremated. In fact, Melanie was out back scattering the ashes around the base of the old Tulip Tree when the realtor brought the first potential buyers through. Farmington wasn't exactly a hot real estate market, but Melanie needed the headache of owning the house gone more than she needed the money. It was priced to sell, and the first group to come through made an offer the exact same evening. Melanie accepted it. She would have accepted five bucks if that was what they offered. *What the house deserved,* she thought, *was to suffer the same fate as the television.* If she could have she'd have knocked it flat with the sledgehammer. She just didn't have the physical strength, at least not yet. Plus she was worried about it falling on her head.

During the thirty days Melanie had to stick around clearing out the house and waiting for the deal to close, she kept it secret that she had won anything. She just swiped her ATM card when she shopped and let the money deduct from the over five-hundred-thousand dollar balance in her account.

With her checkbook in hand, she strolled back over to Doss Street and banged on the front door of one of the houses. An old man answered the door. He was frighteningly thin and had to hold himself up with a cane. Some thin wisps of black hair snuck out from underneath a ball cap that said "I like to see a nice broad smile, especially when she's smiling at me."

"Can I help you, miss?" he said in a voice that was rendered scratchy and quiet from a lifetime of smoking cigarettes.

"I want to buy your Winnebago," said Melanie, making damn sure she didn't smile. "How much do you want for it?"

The man sucked in his lips. He had no teeth at all. If he had dentures, he wasn't wearing them that today.

"You want to buy the Winnie?" he repeated. "Let me get my coat."

The Winnebago was a late seventies ITASCA C25A. Its original white paint had turned creamy, but it wasn't in bad shape. The old man kept it parked underneath a large canopy. The big motor only had ninety thousand and change on it, but the inside of the camper seemed well worn. Apparently the old man's nephew had lived in it for several years until he got picked up by a fracking company in Oklahoma. The nephew was a gear-head and kept the engine running great, but he was hard on the interior. Most of the upholstery was torn. There was a significant crack in the front windshield. The toilet seemed to function, but the tank hadn't been emptied in who knows how long. It smelled like shit and death. There was a hot water heater and an oven all running on propane. Both systems were rusty but functioning. The mattress was going to have to go. It was as thin as a quilt. Melanie found an old copy of the porno rag *Plumpers* stashed beneath it.

"I'll hang onto that," said the old man, who flashed a faint smile and then let his eyes wander over Melanie's very full figure.

"I'm not touching it," said Melanie. "What are you asking for this thing?"

"It's worth a lot, you know."

"To who?"

"Well, it's not easy to find one from this era that runs this well."

"The interior is disgusting."

"Lot of memories have been made in here."

"Please don't tell me anymore. How much are you asking?"

"Well," he puckered his gums a few times while thinking, "I'd be willing to let her go for six-thousand. If you promise to take good care of her."

"I'll give you five-thousand."

"Sold."

After the check cleared and the keys were exchanged, Melanie dropped it off at Dave's RV Center outside of St. Louis to have the interior redone. When she got back to Farmington, she threw out all of the food in the house and embarked on a strict exercise routine.

Melanie had more than enough money to do what most of the overweight Missouri brass did: have their excess fat sucked out by a plastic surgeon. After which they would binge on new clothing that wouldn't fit for long as their eating habits translated to more cellulose and more trips to the sympathetic doctor. Melanie was going to get herself into shape old school. She started jogging first thing in the morning. The first few attempts left her winded before reaching the corner. By the time the house closed, she was running three miles before breakfast everyday. She had abandoned sweets and shifted toward one of those high protein/low-carb diets that were all the rage. She had even been taking a beginner's yoga class three nights a week.

It was full blown spring when a vibrant Melanie, down twenty pounds and wearing designer sunglasses, drove the spruced up Winnie south on Route 67 toward Greenville knowing exactly where she was headed: anywhere the fuck else.

On a postcard day in late August, Melanie watched the sun rise and set from the beach on Key West. The back end of the Winnie was peppered with bumper stickers from truck stops all over the southeast, still running like a top. The interior of the RV had all new upholstery and was filling up with knick-knacks from her travels: a Disney World snow globe, a bronze bust of Elvis Presley, a potholder shaped like Texas. It always smelled like birthday cake inside because of the air freshener that she hung from the rearview.

Melanie was looking and feeling her undisputed best. The awkward red hair that she grew up with had turned cantaloupe from all the sun she'd been getting. Not only that, it was thicker and longer than she'd ever managed to grow it. Thanks, no doubt, to the array of vitamins that she had recently started taking after an herbalist that she befriended in Savannah convinced her of their value. It wasn't just Melanie's hair either. Her skin was finally an even healthy peach tone. Her watery blue eyes stood out more than they ever used to. A couple of trips to the dentist in Santa Fe left her with teeth that were finally parallel and white as fresh snow. She was mostly avoiding alcohol, unless it seemed like a special social occasion (she didn't want to be prudish), but it messed with the morning runs she still dutifully took. Seeking out yoga studios as she traveled helped her make a few friends and exposed her to more styles of teaching. Her breath and heart rate had calmed, and her flexibility had increased. Melanie used her generous food budget to seek out top-quality produce at the grocery stores and always steered clear of fried foods and sugars if she splurged and ate out. She wasn't what anyone would call skinny yet, but she had broken the two-hundred pound barrier, and she had broken it the hard way. She was still plump. But it was a taut, toned, and confident plumpness, sporting bright white choppers and soft hair the color of ripe fruit. She had abandoned the loose-fitting sweatpants and flannels that she used to live in. Her new wardrobe consisted of tighter, hipper outfits that showed off the perfect roundness of her rear end and her boobs. Melanie was sexy.

She decided that arriving at the southeastern most tip of the country was significant enough cause for celebration. During the perfect twilight weather of that glorious summer evening, she drank an unknown number of margaritas and sang an off-key rendition of The Steve Miller Band's *Abracadabra* at a bar whose name she'll never recall. Fortunately the audience was as drunk as she was, and she left the stage to a standing ovation. She even got an offer to park her Winnie for the night in the driveway of a local boat captain named Jack. By the time she woke up in Jack's bed, he was long gone. Had to leave before four to make preparations for a sport fishing charter that shoved off before first light. There was a friendly note by the bed but no phone number or invitation to return. Melanie didn't care. The boys back in Farmington would have used a blind heifer before using her. It was just another boost to her waxing self esteem. She slept in his bed until 8:30, found a place to get a bagel with peanut butter and a cup of coffee, and then went and treated herself to a pedicure.

Tranquil as the Keys are, it can be difficult and expensive to find somewhere to pass the starry nights, even in an RV. Melanie lucked into a late cancellation at The Big Pine Key Fishing Lodge, and they parked her next to a Isuzu Pup tugging a badly oxidized mid-1960's Airstream trailer. It belonged to a high school librarian named Betty, who was starting the process of packing up her things and heading back north to Cherry Hill, New Jersey for another long cold winter. The two of them hit it right off.

"Do you have any interest in this face cream? I just bought it for eleven bucks, but all it's doing is clogging my pores and making me break out into zits like a damn adolescent," asked Betty, before introducing herself.

"If all it does is clog up your pores, why would I want it?"

"It's just because of the menopause, I think. It's making my hormones get all screwy. You'll be fine. You're nowhere near as old as I am."

"I bet that isn't true. You look like you're in great shape. I'd be stunned to hear that you're forty."

"Nice try, dumpling. More like fifty-eight," Betty scrunched her face up as she said this.

"I'm stunned. I don't believe it. You look fantastic."

"All right, all right, keep talking," said Betty. The two of them had a big laugh and finally introduced themselves.

"So," asked Melanie, "what's to do to here at the Big Pine Key Fishing Lodge?"

"I assume you mean besides fishing."

"Yeah, I don't really like killing innocent creatures."

"Well there aren't any innocent creatures in Florida, so you might as well shoot from the hip, Melanie." They laughed again. "No seriously, it isn't too bad. Especially during the day when most of the men are out chasing marlin in their gas guzzling boats. There's a bridge group and a couple of book clubs." Betty whispered the next part, "there's even a Christian one of you're into that kind of thing." Melanie shook her head. Despite being from the Bible Belt, she didn't believe in God. As far as she was concerned, no one but the Powerball commission had ever done a damn thing for her. If she was going to pray, she would pray to them. Fuck God. "Good," chuckled Bettie. "Me either. The pool is nice and so is the hot tub. I like reading novels in the lounge chairs and working on my tan." This much was obvious; Betty was a little on the leathery side. "On Wednesdays at four there's a yoga class in the commons building."

"Really, I love to do yoga. Do you go?"

"Sure do. It's kind of an old farts' version of yoga, so don't expect too much. But the instructor is fantastic. He's French, and I think he knows all kinds of martial arts and Tai Chi as well. His name is Lyle."

"Is he handsome?"

"Well, he's in great shape. Dark-skinned with long black hair. Kind of on the short side though. And you know what that translates to?" Betty lifted up her eyebrows and chuckled. "Although there are a few interesting stories about him that circulate."

"Tell me."

"I heard that he can double in size."

"You're pulling my leg."

"I'm not. Peg and Joan told me, so I'm pretty sure it's true. Some thugs tried to jump him in Tampa, and he doubled in size. Left two of them on the street with broken arms and legs. It has something to do with his chi."

"His what?"

"His chi. Listen, I wasn't there, dumpling, so I can't confirm the story, but you know what I did see?"

"What's that?'

"We were in class one day, doing a sun salutation, when Mr. Watson's Chihuahua came storming into the room and bit Lyle in the calf. Lyle didn't even stop moving for a second. By the time he returned to standing pose, the dog was long gone. It had run off terrified. Then Lyle reached down and pulled one of the dog's canine teeth out of his calf, root and all. Do you believe that? The dog tried to bite him in the leg, and the leg was stronger than the tooth. After class, Lyle gave the tooth back to Mr. Watson, and the vet over on Grassy Key was able to reattach it. Shit, I nearly forgot. It's Wednesday. We have to go. I have an extra mat if you need to borrow one."

"I've got a mat," said Melanie, still looking a little doubtful. "It's just not really a good day for me."

"Are you on your moon, dumpling? I wouldn't let that stop me. Not like it's even an issue anymore."

"No, I'm actually not."

"Why the heck not, then?"

Melanie leaned in close so that she could disclose the following information in secret. The gesture strengthened the developing bond between the two women. "I just got a tattoo," whispered Melanie.

"You didn't?"

"I did," Melanie blushed. "It's my first one."

"Well let me see it, dumpling," said Betty.

Melanie pulled down on the collar of her V-neck. Underneath it she was wearing the top half of a bikini. From the shadowy heart of Melanie's cleavage, a phoenix rose from the ashes. It looked exactly like the sort of thing that you'd see on the hood of an old Pontiac Trans-Am. The hot red color that the tattoo artist used for the bird would probably mellow over time. It was outlined in thick black. At the moment, it had a lot of bling. Melanie looked into the eyes of her new friend with that desperate feeling that only a person who just accidentally got a horrific tattoo, tremendous in scale, and in a highly visible location could possibly understand. Fortunately for Melanie, Betty was a wizard with people's emotions. Her saggy jaw dropped and her eyes rendered the perfect balance between bewilderment and envy.

"It's awesome," she said. "Is that supposed to be like, the new you?"

"I've been going through a lot of changes lately."

"I want to hear all about it, dumpling. But I don't see why you'd need to miss the yoga class. Just put something on it to keep it moist. I think I got some bag balm if you need something to borrow. Then keep it out of the sun while it heals."

"You seem to know more about tattoos than I do."

"Are you kidding me? I got two boys, and they're both covered in them. My oldest is a plumber, and he's got a tattoo of a damn plunger on his forearm. A plunger. Can you even believe it? Look, I'm going to take my nap. When I get up, we'll walk over to yoga together."

Just before four, Betty knocked on the door of the Winnie. She was dressed in her yoga gear. Mostly tight black but not tight enough to hide the fact that her skin was getting loose everywhere. She had a visor on and hot pink wristbands.

Melanie had also gotten in a nap and a shower, and she felt fine and looked even finer. She'd been getting plenty of fresh air. Not knowing where she was headed or who she was going to run into on any given day had filled her with a youthfulness she'd honestly never known. Sometimes she had to force herself to admit that the she and the Melanie who ate thousands of frozen dinners while watching Pat Sajak with her agoraphobic mother were the same person. She danced now. Not too well but she was getting better. It was all about not working too hard. It was about not thinking too much. She had acquired a glow, combined with a body that was curvy and ripe. Like a melon. Like a cantaloupe. A soothing fleshy orange tone, firm but yielding, juicy without being messy, sweet without making the teeth hurt. Melanie wore red spandex tights that looked like they were designed just for her. They looked good with her wild red toenails and her freshly washed hair. She was wearing a stretchy white top. The tattoo wasn't easily visible but it wasn't hidden either. Melanie was learning to wear it well. Over her shoulder, she carried a top-loading mat bag. In it, she carried the spongy blue mat that she liked and her water bottle.

"There's something else I forgot to tell you about the teacher," said Betty as they walked toward where the class was going to be.

"Is he flirty?"

"He can be. He's also a big Elvis fan. Every class he teaches, he leaves a mat on the floor for Elvis to practice on, in case he shows up. From time to time, he'll tell the class to envision Elvis doing yoga with perfect form on the empty mat. It's a little weird at first, but you get used to it. It even helps in an odd way."

"I love Elvis."

"Me too, dumpling."

"The teacher sounds like a nut."

"It's just Florida."

Betty introduced Melanie to Lyle at the beginning of the class while the other students were all laying out their mats. It was all women in the room besides Lyle, and potentially the ghost of Elvis. Lyle was handsome, Betty wasn't kidding. He had hypnotic dark eyes. Neat black hair was tied back and hung almost down to his waist. He had a salt and pepper beard, and all of his facial features were so relaxed that he had hardly any wrinkles, except around the corners of his mouth. Probably he laughed a lot. His age was anyone's guess. He repeated Melanie's name in an accent that retained only the slightest trace of his native French.

"Melanie," he said, "like a melon. Welcome to yoga. Have you ever practiced before?"

"I have been to some classes but only recently. I'm kind of getting into it."

"That's wonderful," he said. "It's very nice to meet you." Lyle wasn't quite dressed like a yogi. A gold choker overlapped his unmarked black T-shirt. His pants were brown canvas and baggy, the kind martial art fighters tend to wear. It was hard to tell how short he really was at first because he was seated in a full lotus pose with his spine ramrod straight. He was very fit but not in the kind of way that would turn heads on the beaches south of Miami. His shoulders were narrow but well-formed, his chest looked powerful but smaller than his waist. It was almost possible to confuse him for fat. What he had was an extraordinarily strong core attached to limbs that were at once fluid and graceful and deadly.

Nine ladies showed up for the class. Betty obviously knew them all and shared their names with Melanie, from which she retained a Violet and a Peg and was damn sure that Joan wasn't there because of her sciatica. Lyle had them all begin seated and focusing on their breath.

"You know, I find when I come down here, that you ladies have an easier time then most settling into the relaxed flow of the yoga. Up in the city, everyone is going this way or that way. In class, they are all trying to push themselves into this pose or that pose. I think they'd learn a lot from coming down here and practicing with you ladies. I know Elvis likes it a lot better down here. Don't you, King? Yeah, me too."

"We may not do headstands, but we know how to relax, right girls?"

Melanie laughed along with the rest of the group, even though she wasn't sure if she counted among them. Sure she was part of the RV crowd now. It's just that the other women seemed a lot older than her.

"The key to relaxation, Lyle, is take two vacations a year," Peg went on, "but they've got to be six months a piece."

"Cheers, Peg." Everyone laughed.

"Alright," said Lyle, "I can see that you are all in a feisty mood today. We've got Melanie joining us for the first time. It's a beautiful day with a nice breeze. Let's just all sit here together for a moment and notice the moment."

Outside the big window that most of the students were facing stood a palm tree that was in serious decline. Many of its roots were severed when a plumbing crew trenched a new sewer pipe into the commons building. About five years ago, a new parking lot was installed just on the north side of it and the soil had gotten very compacted. There was a long scar in the trunk from where someone hit it with a boat trailer. It was parched and riddled with dead fronds. Practically begging for a mercy kill.

"Some people would look at that tree and say that it's and ugly tree. Some people might say that it's still a beautiful tree. Me, I don't name it. I just look. We get so caught up in naming everything all the time. There's no need. You have to learn to let it be."

After that, they all sat quiet together for a short while, and then Lyle led the class in a series of neck and shoulder rolls just to get a little loose. Then the group transitioned onto all fours and engaged in a series of cat and cow poses to wake the spine up. Melanie stole a glance around and was impressed. Half the room had to be pushing eighty. But they were all moving with the same supple grace as the charming instructor. He got them to roll over their toes into a position in which the arms and legs are both extended and the butt is thrust well up into the air. It's called a downward dog pose, but Lyle preferred to call it by its Sanskrit name, *Adho Mukha Svanasana*. It's a move that takes a lot of strength in the forearms, and Melanie was blown away that everyone in the room looked so good in it. Everyone, that is, except for Betty. Betty had abandoned the pose for a comfortable seat and chugged thirty-two ounces of purple Vitamin Water in about half a second. Melanie, noticing her friend's sudden distress, bent close to her for a quick talk. Betty was red as a beet.

"I'm having a hot flash," whispered Betty. "I've got to get out of here."

"Should I come with you?" asked Melanie. Frankly she didn't want to. She was really getting into the class and liked Lyle as an instructor. He seemed far superior to anyone else that she had worked with so far.

"No, no. You stay. I'll be fine. I just have to go to the beach and cool off. I'll see you later." Betty apologized for having to leave the class in the middle, claiming that she simply wasn't feeling well. Lyle complimented her for knowing herself and wished her well as she made her exit.

"Yoga can be very intense," said Lyle after Betty had gone. "Sometimes it's too intense and what our bodies really need is to rest. It's the resting in between the postures when yoga has its true benefit."

The next forty-five minutes was filled with a short series of standing poses, forward folds, and some simple vinyasas. The class finished up with a few gentle floor twists, the chanting of three Oms together, and a lengthy dead man's during which Lyle played the harmonium. After he finished playing, but before releasing the women from the trance that he had led them into, he swung by Melanie's mat while her eyes were closed.

"Hang back after class, will ya?" he whispered into her ear. And then he took up his position at the front of the room again. "Let's start to slowly bring ourselves back into this space," he said, "in case you happen to have drifted off. I don't know if some of you have gone inside your minds to India or Africa, or driven one of your RVs over to California. All I know is that right now at this moment, you shouldn't be making any plans. Remember, nothing ever happens in the future. There is only what is happening in the now. You need to learn the art of slowing down. Although I know that you ladies are better at that than most. Up in Tampa, I've got people answering their cell phones during class. It was wonderful to see you all as usual. I'll be back again next week. Namaste, ladies."

"Namaste," said the class.

People started drinking from their water bottles and rolling up their mats. A few of the ladies invited Lyle to their trailers for a happy hour cocktail.

"Thank you, ladies, but I don't drink. I wish I could."

Melanie sort of loitered on her mat alternately practicing asanas and trying to keep her heart rate under 200. Eventually the room emptied out, and it was just the two of them left in there. Lyle glided across the white tile floor and arched backward until his hands hit the ground. From there, he lifted his legs one at a time into a handstand, held it, and breathed. Then he settled his legs on the floor and came into a yogic squat right in front of where Melanie was still sitting on her mat.

"Hey," said Lyle, "what do you say you and I take a walk down to the beach? I could use some nourishment."

"Well, that sounds fun, but I'm all sweaty from the class."

"Who cares? Sweat is wonderful," Lyle leaned into Melanie, stretched his tongue way out, and lapped up several rivulets of perspiration between her triceps and her armpit. Melanie blushed like a tangerine. "Let's go," said Lyle.

*

"Oh my, you really are flexible," the voice yanked Betty out of a deep sleep. She was lying at the edge of the pine forest with a cool towel draped over her eyes, just uphill from a deserted stretch of sandy white beach. The sun was going down behind the forest, and a couple was approaching on the path that led through the dunes. Betty kept still in the shadows and let them pass. She felt a little bit better but still dizzy and sweating despite the fact that the day was cooling off. Once she felt like the couple was far enough toward the water's edge, she risked taking the wet towel away from her eyes to get a peek at who it was, and she nearly swallowed her tongue. It was the yoga instructor Lyle, acting sort of cozy-like with the new girl from Missouri. She was happy for Melanie, and then fury washed over her. She was blind with envy. Of course he would go for the younger girl, even if she was heavyset. What were they about to do? Skinny dip in the moonlight? Have sex on the beach?

Then Betty noticed something very peculiar about Lyle. Something had happened to his legs. They had essentially fused together and tapered, not to feet, but a stack of menacing black rings. Lyle wasn't so much cozying up to Melanie as he was slithering around her. Betty got a good look at Melanie's face. The poor girl looked scared. Lyle looked more or less the way he always did, like a poised coil of muscle. He still looked charming and as handsome as ever. He still had the long black ponytail.

Lyle unwrapped himself from Melanie and made little S-turns with his torso in the sand, as though he was warming himself up. Betty couldn't say whether his shoulders or his arms disappeared next. It all seemed to happen at the same time. Lyle's hands melted into his hips and then the whole region lost its taper. Lyle's neck was gone. He had morphed into an imposing green-black snake that was winding itself up and steadying for a strike.

The sun's last rays lit Melanie's face up, and she looked surprisingly relaxed. A pair of brown pelicans flew overhead without pausing to take notice of anything but the surface of the sea. Betty didn't really know anything about the cute girl on her own in the clunky Winnebago, but she did get a warm feeling that where she was during that sunset was much nicer than where she had started out from. Welcome to the Keys. If only there was still time to share a margarita together. But there wasn't.

Lyle wasn't noticing any of the sweetness that Betty was when he eyed his prey. The only things he saw were biomass and heat, and perhaps there was still a small part of his unconscious mind that recalled her having a particularly juicy quality. His hair was gone now and so was the beard, replaced with salt and pepper scales. The gold choker snapped when the neck thickened and was lying on its own in the sand. Four of Lyle's bright white teeth stretched out into a viscous fangs and oozed something that could only be poison. His elastic body thrust itself at Melanie with incredible force, wrapping itself thrice around her and squeezing. Blueberry yogurt and granola shot out of Melanie's mouth like a spume. The snake man squeezed harder, and Melanie's face turned from orange to purple to blue to lifeless. She didn't appear to put up any type of a fight. Betty sat watching the scene, frozen in terror, but less in disbelief than you might imagine. Apparently there was some truth to the stories about Lyle.

Only after the poor girl's soul had flown off with the pelicans did the snake man release his grip. Melanie collapsed onto the soft sand, and Lyle circled her a few times, letting his forked tongue dance along the sweaty skin of his victim. It sort of occurred to Betty that even though she was cloaked from view and had the favorable light, she was alone on a beach with a fresh corpse and a shape-shifting yoga instructor who had just turned into an asphyxiator right before her eyes. She thought for a moment it might be best to run. But it also could have been dangerous. Plus, if we are being completely honest, she wanted to see what was going to happen next. A pair of hopeful buzzards appeared doing lazy circles in the sky just overhead. The snake man hissed at them and they flew off. Then he unhinged his jaw.

The snake man began the process of swallowing Melanie whole by the head. He sunk his four fangs into the pudgy fat beneath her jawbone and milked his powerful upper body up over her face. Betty saw all of that lovely hair disappear like water going down a drain. With his tail, the snake man reached around and slit Melanie's white yoga top down the center, allowing her big beautiful breasts to fall out to the sides and exposing her new tattoo to the first stars of the night. The snake man's forked tongue emerged again and took its time sliding back and forth along the tattoo, occasionally meandering to the right or to the left to tickle one of the orange nipples. The snake man widened again, unhooked his jaws and slid them down to the narrower region below Melanie's ribs in one deft move. *Disgusting as it is beautiful,* thought Betty.

What little light there was glinted for just a second off of a belly button ring that Melanie had gotten somewhere in her travels. It made Betty sad. Something about the tattoo and the piercing together. She was glad that at least she got to see them and how good they looked on her, and how good the red spandex pants still looked on her. Underneath those pants was a pair of striped cotton panties from Victoria's Secret, a wild tuft of pumpkin-colored pubic hair in desperate need of a trim, and a wad of Preparation H that was interfacing with a variety of other bodily fluids in her butt crack. Lyle got all of that and down to her knees in his next bite.

In a strange way, Betty felt sad that this terrifying spectacle was nearly complete. She felt like a witness to another dimension or a whole new universe that had been forever existing beside her. Lyle could have finished Melanie off in another bite, but he probably wanted to savor the moment as well. He moved his jaws down to Melanie's ankles and left only her feet dangling out of his mouth. Clydine, the adorable aesthetician who just earlier that morning painted Melanie's toenails fire engine red with silver swirls, would have likely been touched to know that those nails were the last parts of Melanie to exist in this world. And then the snake man ate those too. After that he looked heavy and tired. And it was dark enough that Betty was comfortable sneaking away. At least the hot flash was over.

✕◊✕◊✕ ✕◊✕◊✕ ✕◊✕◊✕ ✕◊✕

About the Author

Douglas Andrew Smith is a fiction writer living in the Pacific Northwest region of the United States. He holds a bachelor's degree from The Evergreen State College and an MFA from Goddard College.

Ozzy Tate's Toe

Daniel Henshaw

Day 1: March 22 - Saturday Afternoon

"Can you actually remember what Ozzy's toe is like?" Tez was amazed at what Matthew had just proposed. Still, Matthew remained defiant. "I'm not fazed by it. I can take him in a toe war."

The trio—Ozzy, Tez, and Matthew—had been close friends since their school days and getting together for drinks on a Saturday afternoon was a weekly ritual. A mini March heat wave had sent temperatures soaring into the twenties, something of a sensation for northern England, and everyone had gotten into a premature summer mind-set: shorts and sandals were visible on every street. On this particular Saturday, the group had quite purposely selected the Skegwood pub with the best beer garden, The French Horn. Sitting on a sun-drenched plot of grass seemed to require all customers to drink cider of some guise or other, and this group was no exception: apple cider, pear cider, berry cider, mango cider, ginger cider, curry cider, baked bean cider, and so on.

The topics of conversation had developed as fluently as they usually did with a range of questions being raised.

Which footballer has the funniest name?

What would win in a fight between a Reliant Robin and a Lada?

Does cider count toward your five-a-day?

Which film was better: Star Cry 1 *or* Star Cry 3*?*

Do girls get naturally fatter during their periods?

Other burning issues had been debated, too. However, the discussions ended at the first proposal of a thumb war. Matthew loved them. He was obsessed with them. And he took them seriously. If Matthew had been as competitive with his work at school as he was during a thumb war, he'd have been a straight-A student. Instead, he was expelled for fighting a teacher and left school with little more than a reputation as a rogue. The thumb wars on this March afternoon were no different to any other time; Matthew, as usual, beat Tez and Ozzy with relative ease. His thumb seemed almost double-jointed, and it gave him a huge advantage.

"How about a toe war then?" suggested Ozzy, the tallest of the group by some distance.

Matthew was on his sixth rhubarb cider and felt fired up. "Yes! Now we're talking!"

No matter how great Matthew was at thumb wars, Tez had every confidence that he'd lose to Ozzy in a toe war as Ozzy Tate's toe had gained something of a reputation within the local community. Had Ozzy's biggest toe been an average size, he would probably have been able to fit his feet into a size 11 shoe. However, his largest toe was so large that he actually needed to wear size 19 shoes!

"I say," said Ozzy, which was a phrase—almost like an uncontrollable tick—that he always used before the announcement of some great, unimportant fact. "Did you know that toe wrestling almost became an Olympic sport in 1997?"

"Shut up," dismissed Matthew.

"I swear to God," which was a irrelevant thing to do because Ozzy Tate didn't believe in God, "it was proposed, but the Olympic committee, or whatever they're called, rejected it. Bastards! Just think, I could be an Olympic champion at something!"

"Are you definitely good at toe wrestling then?" asked Tez.

"Dunno, never done it before."

Ozzy had always been proud of his big toe. When he was six years old, he had entered a local art competition with the help of his mum; he had produced a huge, detailed painting of a butterfly, some wonderfully shaped pottery, and a truly original collage made from *Skittles*. To much excitement, the mayor had come along to judge the competition with his glistening gold chains draped around his shoulders. When he arrived at Ozzy's collection of artwork, he had asked the young boy what he was most proud of.

"My toe!" Ozzy had replied.

Even in his older years, Ozzy was not shy about displaying his large toe in public either; it made him feel unique, special. The teenage years were the worst. With everyone vying for attention and always trying to be different, Ozzy would just get his toe out: showing the staff in Tesco, scaring small children in the park, or asking intoxicated girls to suck it. For the sake of attention, Ozzy would do anything with his rather interesting toe. It had been used as a shadow puppet, a totem pole, and even a temporary, makeshift Christmas tree. But now, for the first time, it was about to engage in toe warfare.

As Ozzy removed his sock, a couple of girls nearby took notice. "Oh my god! Look at the size of his toe!" Kirsty and Lara grabbed their drinks and came over. They were obviously immediately impressed by Matthew's bravado and became engrossed in the ensuing toe wars. However, try as he might, Matthew—the King of Thumb Wars—could not compete when it came to toes. As Tez had predicted, Ozzy's toe was just too big. It was David vs. Goliath, and this time Goliath won. Kirsty and Lara slurped their turnip ciders as they giggled away. Matthew and Ozzy exchanged banter, and the girls loved their sense of humour.

"You two are so funny," they repeated on numerous occasions.

"Your toe is amazing!" screeched Lara, slurring her words ever so slightly. "Look at how it can grip his whole foot!"

Ozzy smiled smugly. "That's nothing. Watch this." Before Lara had time to think, Ozzy had gripped hold of her pint glass—with his toe!—and taken a drink. The girls watched with open mouths, stared at each other, and then cheered.

Meanwhile, Tez, who didn't compete in the toe wars, had become a little restless. *I have a beautiful fiancé at home,* he thought to himself. *Why would I want to hang around with these cheap tarts?* After finishing his final horseradish cider, he made a polite excuse and parted company with his two old friends. Tez's departure made room for Kirsty and Lara to move in a little closer to the remaining lads.

"My friends call me Cock-Thirsty Kirsty," Kirsty told Matt.

"And I'm Loose Lara," stated Lara proudly, winking at Ozzy.

Matthew and Ozzy were loving the attention. They, unlike Tez, did not have a beautiful fiancé to go home to, just a shared flat, which they had affectionately named The Love Nest, and a collection of dirty magazines with most of the pages stuck together. Ozzy had always done okay with the ladies. While he wasn't strikingly attractive, with his unstyled, wavy hair and the out-of-season clothes that he'd picked up in the sales, his bright, blue eyes were honest and his straight, white teeth projected the kind smile that most girls could warm to.

Lara, feeling the effects of her eighth turnip cider, stroked Ozzy's chest. Her shabbily painted finger nails ran along the outside of an image on his T-shirt—little did she know that this was the emblem of his favourite sci-fi movie, *Star Cry 3*—and then she whispered seductively into his ear. "I'd love to know what else you can do with that toe."

"Come back to The Love Nest and you might find out." Without hesitating, Ozzy moved in for the kiss and was instantly reminded how amazing it was to feel a girl's soft tongue against his. He pressed his hand against her firm breast. Lara didn't object, and Ozzy knew that he was in business.

"I'll call us a taxi," suggested Lara.

What Ozzy didn't know was that his next few words would change his life forever.

"No, let's walk back over the bridge."

Day 1: March 22 - Saturday Night

Getting back to The Love Nest left the foursome with a dilemma. It meant either a ten-minute taxi ride, at an extortionate cost, or a five-minute walk. The reason for this bizarre situation was due to Skegwood's irregular shape. The town was built at the top of a tremendously steep hill, which was shaped like a horseshoe. From The French Horn pub, The Love Nest was on the opposite side of the town's obsolete bridge, Aqueduct Drop. Although it was deemed unsafe for cars by the local council, the bridge could be walked across in five minutes, if the weather was reasonable. To get to the other side of town in a car meant driving along the shape of the horseshoe, which took about ten minutes.

The reason that the bridge had acquired the name Aqueduct Drop was due to the facts that:

Built in the late 19th Century, the bridge was designed to look like a Roman aqueduct. Hence, the Aqueduct part.

If you fell off the edge, which a number of people had done over the last century or so, you faced an enormous drop to the bottom and, most definitely, to your death. Hence, the Drop part.

The bridge had been closed since 1979, becoming rather lonely and derelict. Matthew and Ozzy would cross the bridge every so often, mainly to get to The French Horn or Ozzy's favourite supermarket, Lucarelli's; their delicatessen served the best cheese. Convincing the girls to walk across proved a little more difficult.

"Why can't we just get a taxi?" complained Lara.

"Walking will be far quicker!" Ozzy was at his charming, drunken best. "Just think, the sooner we get there, the sooner we can open that bottle of Southern Comfort that I told you about. I've been saving it for a special occasion, and I can't think of anything more special than you."

"Okay." Lara smiled at his alluring words. "But I'm taking my shoes off before we walk across that bridge! I don't want to fall off there! And my feet are killing me in these heels!"

The fruity foursome climbed over a decrepit gate and staggered along the enormous bridge. At such a height, a light wind inevitably blew the girls' skirts around, and each time it did, the girls screeched a boozy howl of a scream.

Wind blows. Skirts flap. Scream.

Wind blows. Skirts flap. Scream.

Wind blows. Skirts flap. Scream.

Scream. Scream. Scream. But it wasn't the girls this time! Somebody in the distance was screeching. Ozzy and Matthew left the girls behind and sprinted in the direction of the panicked sounds. As they got closer, they could see the figure of a frantic girl. She was hysterically trying to tell the boys something, but the words were leaving her mouth at such a rapid velocity that it was simply gibberish.

"My boyfriend! He fell! He's hanging!" Although the bridge was lit only by the reflected beams of the moon, tears were clearly streaming from her eyes, and she appeared to be dribbling wildly, too.

Matthew and Ozzy approached the edge of the bridge extremely carefully. Was the wind getting stronger? It was a long way down once you got close to the edge. The fallen boy was just visible. He was gripping onto something, and his fingertips were about seven feet below them. Matthew reached his arm down. It was nowhere near the boy. Immediately, he bravely swung himself over the edge and gripped on with his fingers.

"Matt, what are you doing?" Ozzy thought his friend was insane.

Matthew dipped his feet and stretched his toes as far as his could, but the boy's hands were still a good twelve inches away. He pulled himself back onto the bridge. "You'll have to do it," he said, pointing at Ozzy.

"No way! I say, I'm not hanging over the side of this bridge."

By this time, Loose Lara and Cock-Thirsty Kirsty had caught up. "What's going on?"

Matthew explained the situation and then turned to Ozzy. "You're loads taller than me, you'll be able to reach him!"

The girls agreed. "You have to do it, Ozzy! There's somebody's life at stake here."

The boy's girlfriend was getting more frantic by the second. Spit dribbled from her chin.

Ozzy had always loved to be the center of attention; he was an extrovert. When he lived in Australia for a while, he had once turned up at a party dressed as a woman. Nobody else had been in fancy dress, but he loved being different, for everyone to be talking about him, to have all eyes on him. All eyes were on him right now, but this was the scariest thing Ozzy had ever done. He felt sick, truly sick. His heart wasn't beating; it was thrashing around somewhere between his throat and his stomach. This could be it; he could die right now. On this warm March night, Oslo Percy Tate felt like he was on the verge of death. And for what? Just to *try* to save somebody's life. *Try*. He may not even succeed. But he had to. Ozzy knew that he had to do it. There were girls watching, after all.

He approached the edge slowly. The edge of the bridge—possibly the edge of his life. For a brief moment, he thought about his mum and how much he loved her. His mum was a free spirit, a bit of hippy. She was one who had given him this ridiculous name— Oslo—because he'd been conceived in Norway's capital city. She told Ozzy this fact when he was just six years old; she was that kind of mother—very open with her children. Ozzy's brother was called Joshua; he had been conceived while U2's *Joshua Tree* was playing from the tape deck. Ozzy loved his mum more than anyone. And, right now as he peered over the edge of the bridge, he wanted to be with her instead. His hands shook furiously as he lowered himself; the sickness in his stomach was inclined to be at vomiting point at any second. He lowered himself further, gripping tightly to the edge of the bridge. He stretched his body, his whole body. There must have been over seven feet of Ozzy Tate hanging over the edge of Aqueduct Drop. Suddenly, he felt the boy's fingers on his shoes. But, almost as quickly, they seemed to let go. Again, they grabbed. But, again, they let go. Ozzy didn't want to look down. He really didn't. But he needed to know what was happening. He looked. The fallen boy was trying to grab his foot but he couldn't get any purchase on the slippery shoe. Ozzy knew exactly what to do. He pulled himself back onto the bridge.

"WHAT ARE YOU DOING?" The boy's girlfriend now looked like she was possessed.

Ozzy ignored her cries and immediately set about taking off his shoes and socks. Without any hesitation this time, he lowered himself over the edge and stretched out his entire body. As soon as he felt the boy's fingers on his big toe, he grabbed it powerfully. His toe's grip was incredibly strong, like that of a chimpanzee.

Ozzy shouted to the group on the bridge. "Pull me!"

Holding on to the boy's hand with his toe, Ozzy was heaved back onto the bridge, and, with every ounce of strength he had in his leg, he dragged the boy back to safety, into the weeping arms of his girlfriend.

While this had been going on, Loose Lara had called everyone: the fire service, ambulance, police, helicopter rescue, mountain rescue, lifeboats, RSPCA, Children in Need. Then, as soon as she saw Ozzy back on the bridge, she embraced him in a tight hug. "You're a hero! You saved his life! You're a hero!" After another hug, she got back on the phone: BBC, ITV, Channel 4, Sky News, CNN, HBO, Disney Channel. Everyone needed to know about Ozzy Tate's big toe! And, over the next couple of days, everybody did.

Day 2: March 23ʳᵈ - Sunday Morning

Alone, Ozzy Tate returned to The Love Nest around 10 a.m. Sunday morning. The night's events had left him wired, and there was no way he could go to bed, despite his lack of sleep. He reached into the cupboard and grabbed the bottle of Southern Comfort that he'd been saving since Christmas.

"I say, sorry Lara, but this really *is* a special occasion!" he said to himself in his empty flat. Ozzy poured himself half a pint of the sweet golden liquor. "It's not every day that you save somebody's life!" He gulped the drink down in one, hoping that it would soothe his mind towards tiredness.

Once the police, fire service, and ambulance had arrived on Aqueduct Drop, it wasn't long before the first member of the press made it onto the scene. The first was a journalist from the local newspaper.

"This won't be in time for tomorrow's edition, but it'll be front-page news on Monday!" she had told Ozzy gleefully.

After that came a reporter from the local radio station and once her report had gone live, the whole world appeared to descend on the bridge. Local newspapers, local radio, local TV, then local people with their camera phones. Then the national papers arrived, national radio, and national TV. It was mayhem! Everybody wanted to talk to the hero. Everybody wanted a piece of his amazing toe. Before he knew it, Ozzy was stood in front of a Sky News camera, thumbs up, smiling and waving his toe to millions around the world.

After hours of interviews with police and the media, Ozzy eventually made his escape. Matthew had decided against going home. Instead, he was going to return to the pub in order to tell the story of how he and his best friend's toe saved somebody's life.

Ozzy poured a second glass of Southern Comfort and collapsed on the sofa. He turned on the TV to see his stupid beaming smile slapped across the screen.

"I say, BBC!" he laughed.

Beneath the images of his face, were the words: HUGE TOE SAVES LIFE! Within half an hour, he'd seen his face on nineteen different television channels including *Al Jazeera* and *Russia Today*. All the while, his phone hadn't stopped vibrating. He refused to look at it. Amazing how people only want to know you when you're in the spotlight. After getting a little tired of the TV, he turned on his laptop and typed his name into Google: hundreds and hundreds of pages about the incident last night. It hadn't even been twelve hours! Then he looked himself up on YouTube. Again, there were hundreds of videos. They all had different titles.

Ozzy Tate—Toe Hero
Toe Saves Life
Man Rescues Boy With Toe
Amazing Toe Story
Huge Toe Saves Boy
UK Man—Massive Toe
Look At This Freaky Toe

Ozzy's eyes moved away from the screen and focused on his toes at the opposite end of the sofa.

"I thought that I saved the day," he slurred, wriggling his toe, "but I guess they're more interested in you." He'd always loved his toe and the way that it made him different. However, all of a sudden, the toe was becoming a celebrity in its own right. Next, he logged into Twitter. Unsurprisingly, Ozzy had hundreds of notifications.

Matthew @djmattywires
My best friend @bigtoeOzzy saved someone's life with his toe last night! #hero #supertoe

Tez @terrychuck13
@djmattywires @bigtoeOzzy WHAT?!? How did I miss this? What happened? Your toe is awesome Ozzy! #hero #supertoe

Dan @flavadan
@bigtoeOzzy just saw you on the news man! You and your toe are clearly better than batman lol! #hero #supertoe

Cez @cerilooker11
@bigtoeOzzy saving lives with ur toe? They should make a movie about dat #supertoe

Husss Sandwich Co @HusssSandwichCo

@bigtoeOzzy COOL story man! If you ever hit New York I'll do you a free sandwich! #hero #supertoe

Poonam @poonammavji

@bigtoeOzzy pleeeease bring your toe to delhi and take part in India's Got Talent!!! Your toe is amazing! I love it! #supertoe

Ozzy continued reading. The messages went on. People had been tweeting him from all corners of the globe: India, America, Japan, Brazil, Zimbabwe, Argentina, Malawi. Ozzy didn't even know where Malawi was! Amazingly, #supertoe was trending worldwide, which meant that it was one of the most popular topics in the world.

Ozzy's vacant gaze into his laptop screen was broken by a knock at the door. Who could this be? More media? Perhaps, it was one of the locals pretending to be his friend. Ozzy thought about ignoring it and pretending he was out. Another knock. Ozzy tip-toed over to the door and peeked out of the nearby window. His heart skipped a beat. It was his ex-girlfriend, Becky. Ozzy glanced despairingly at the mirror. To say that he looked like a zombie would probably be offensive to the undead; his panda-like eyes had dark rings, his wavy hair was out of control, and his teeth felt like they had hairs growing on them. He quickly dashed to the bathroom, splashed his face with water, and swilled some mouthwash around the back of his throat.

Things had ended quite badly with Becky; she had wanted to settle down and have kids whereas Ozzy had wanted to push his body to limits of the party lifestyle. Too many nights without coming home and too many embarrassing stories revealed between weekends meant that Becky couldn't take it anymore. She moved back in with her parents while Ozzy moved in with Matthew.

Ozzy took a deep breath and opened the door. In the past, Becky's smile had always made him feel good about the world; now it only made him feel regret. He missed her. When she'd first moved out of the house that they had lived in together, Ozzy had considered suicide on numerous occasions. He'd been incredibly lonely. The boisterous weekends as a single man may have been fun but the days in between were a lonesome, depressing time. He'd begged her to move back in with him, but she couldn't face it. Outrageous drunkenness may have been fun as a teenager but it wasn't conducive to life in a serious relationship. Serious. Why did they have to use that word? Why did it all have to be so serious? All Ozzy had wanted to do was party and have fun. If Becky hadn't been so uptight back then, things could have been different. But they weren't different. Becky had ended it, and now Ozzy wished he'd taken it all a little more…seriously.

At that minute, unlike Ozzy, Becky's skin was glowing. She had clearly had an early night and a good sleep. She looked fresh. She looked healthy. She looked great. "Hello, Becky. Are you all right?"

"I saw you on the TV." Certain noises soothed Ozzy's brain: the purring of his mum's cat, rain pattering on a window, and, of course, the sound of Becky's voice. She noticed his dark, blood-shot eyes. "Have you not been to sleep?"

"No. Don't think I could sleep if I tried!" He showed her into the flat.

"Looks like you're a bit of a star. You're all over Facebook and Twitter and the TV. I can't believe that I'm now standing with the star of the show!" Her cheeky grin was enough to make Ozzy's heart dissolve.

"Who? Me? I say, I'm not the star of the show!"

Becky arched her eyebrow. "You saved somebody's life. Of course, you're the star!"

"Not according to the Internet."

"Well, who is then?"

Ozzy pointed at his feet. "Hashtag super toe!"

Becky laughed; it was an enchanting sound that Ozzy had craved on a daily basis. Before they had eventually broken up, Ozzy had been out on the town every weekend, drinking himself into oblivion. During this time, he'd forgotten about how precious the small things were to him. Now he badly missed sharing a love for those small things: sci-fi movies, pepperoni pizza, jokes about how to wash the dishes correctly. But most of all, he missed Becky's laugh.

The former couple settled down with a cup of tea, and Ozzy retold the tale of the previous evening in his own words. They continued to chat away for the next couple of hours before Ozzy eventually dozed off on the sofa, still wearing the clothes from the previous evening.

Becky grabbed his duvet from the bedroom and covered him up so that he was nice and toasty.

Becky still cared for Ozzy deeply. Did she love him? Of course, she did. If only he hadn't been such a fool in the past. Neglect. That was the only word that sprung to mind when her mind wandered back to the latter days of their relationship. It had been emotional neglect, Ozzy on the town all weekend, drinking himself into a mess. It had gotten to the point where Becky had been too anxious to go to the shops for fear of someone making a comment. "I saw your Ozzy in the Red Lion on Saturday night," they would say. "He threw up and fell over four times before they kicked him out!" She knew he was sorry, had repented for his sins, and now she was ready to forgive him. Becky's hope was that Ozzy's brush with death might help him to focus more prudently on the things that were truly important in his life. And, all being well, she—Becky—would be among those things.

Day 2: March 23 - Sunday Afternoon

When Ozzy woke up five hours later, Becky was still there.

"Get in the shower," she demanded. "We need to leave as soon as possible."

Ozzy attempted to speak, but his words were unintelligible. For half a second, Ozzy had lost all recollection of recent history. Was he still in a relationship with Becky? No, that had definitely ended a long time ago. Did they have sex before he went to sleep? That seemed like an unlikely change of attitude from Becky. Then, all of a sudden, his memories of the past twenty-four hours came flooding back.

Zipping around the flat and getting things ready, Becky was like a five-foot wasp. "We have to be in London by half seven at the latest."

Ozzy managed his first word. "London?" His throat was drier than a stale breadstick.

"Yes. You're going to be on the *Prattle Battle*. I'm just packing a suitcase for you and getting a few bits ready. When you've had a shower and got changed, we can go. Don't worry; I've spoken to your boss, and you're okay to miss work tomorrow. He says your toe is the stuff of legend. I'm going to drive so you can focus on what you're going to say on the show."

"*Prattle Battle?*" Ozzy's mouth was wide open, and his eyes were akin to those of a dog confused by his own fart.

The *Prattle Battle* was a chat show on one of the mainstream TV channels, hosted by the eccentrically camp Allin MacRear. The guests that audiences were mainly interested in were hot, en vogue celebrities doing the rounds of promoting their latest movie, hit single, TV show, book, or range of vegan-ready meals. As well as these guests, there would always be a faded pop star from years ago, who MacRear liked to jibe with sarcastic comments about how well their careers had been going recently. The studio audience always loved it when MacRear made references to the bygone times when the former star was at their peak. The jaded celebrity would giggle along too, just happy to be given some kind of limelight. Finally, there would also be one non-celebrity person on the show each Sunday, someone who had been in the news during the week, and on this particular Sunday, they had contacted Ozzy Tate, the toe-wielding life-saver. While Ozzy had been asleep, Becky had answered the call from the television channel and agreed to get him to their London studios by half past seven.

Still feeling the effects of last night's ciders, Ozzy dragged himself away from the sofa and into the kitchen. His head was pounding and his eyes felt heavy. Shakily, Ozzy heaped two spoonfuls of coffee into his favourite *Star Cry* mug and added two spoons of sugar. Ozzy drank the resulting mud in one quick gulp, and he immediately felt the effects of the caffeine cursing through his bloodstream. Although he'd have preferred to stay on the sofa all day and call for a takeaway later, Ozzy knew that being on a chat show with a big star like Allin MacRear was a once-in-a-lifetime opportunity. He trudged into the shower, hoping to wash away the remaining grubbiness of yesterday's drinking session with Matthew and Tez.

"So," Ozzy was shouting over the din of the shower, "who else is going to be on *Prattle Battle*?"

"Viola Vixen…"

Ozzy squeaked out a laugh. "No way! I'll see if I can find my old calendar for her to sign!" Viola Vixen was a glamour model who seemed to be everywhere during Ozzy's teenage years. At the height of her fame, she was persuaded to record a couple of pop singles, despite having the vocal tone of a peacock.

"Unless you know where it is, we don't have time." Becky was now busy making sandwiches for the journey.

"Who else?"

"Stephen Meadow…"

"I say, I like him, too. He's funny." Stephen Meadow was initially a stand-up comedian, who went on to star on a number of topical panel shows and sitcoms. Recently, he had written, directed, and starred in his very first feature-length movie. "Who else?"

"Erm…Oakland Moore."

Suddenly, the shower's din halted, and there was a silence in the bathroom. Becky heard Ozzy take two heavy steps out of the shower with his size 19 feet. Slowly, dripping water all over the floor, he ghosted from the bathroom with a towel wrapped around his waist.

Ozzy's stare was intense. "What did you just say?"

Becky, knowing how he felt about Oakland Moore, had a huge smile stretched across her face. "Oakland. Bloody. Moore!"

Instantly, Ozzy started jigging around the flat. His towel fell to the ground, and Becky watched as his penis swung around with delight. He was screaming at the top of his voice. "OAKLAND MOORE!"

Oakland Moore was the star of Ozzy's favorite movies, *The Star Cry Trilogy*. Moore had played Kin Lej, the pilot of the coolest spaceship in the universe. In all three of the *Star Cry* movies and in each film, it was Kin who had saved the world. During Ozzy's childhood, his walls had been covered in posters of Kin Lej taking on Wobb-jugglers, Joop-stenchers, and any other filthy aliens that he came across. Upon hearing his name, the bubble of hangover that had surround Ozzy was instantly popped. He sprinted into his bedroom, dressed as quickly as he could, and was ready to go before Becky had finished making her sandwiches.

Becky looked at him. "You're not wearing *that*!" Ozzy had put on his navy *Star Cry* T-shirt.

"Of course I am! It will be funny!"

"It will be cringe-worthy!"

"It will make him laugh!"

"It will freak him out!"

Ozzy trudged to the bedroom and changed his T-shirt, but made sure that he slipped it into his travel bag without Becky noticing.

Day 2: March 23rd - Sunday Evening

Ozzy was eager to get to London to meet his childhood hero, constantly urging Becky to go faster. They arrived just in time. Once inside the channel's enormous building, a studio representative was gibbering away, telling them about the history of the TV station and what the schedule for filming would be. Ozzy, however, was taking none of it in.

In his mind, Ozzy was imagining his meeting with the real Kin Lej: Oakland Moore. Moore, originally from Chicago and now in his sixties, was appearing on the show to promote a new film in which he was playing a corrupt member of the CIA. Ozzy pictured their meeting. They'd be introduced to each other. Ozzy would then make a funny joke, and everyone would burst into hysterics. Oakland would want to know all about Ozzy's life, and he'd find Ozzy's stories really interesting. Ozzy would show his toe on TV and recall some of his funniest toe stories. Oakland would think he was hilarious. After the show, they'd exchange numbers, keep in touch, and become really good friends. Ozzy would go over and stay in Oakland's Malibu beach house. He'd probably be introduced to some of his single actress friends, and Ozzy would spend the summer charming different celebrities into bed. What a life! That was how it played in Ozzy's mind anyway. First though, he had to think of an opening joke to say to his idol.

Mr. Moore or should I just call you Kin? Terrible.

Hello, Mr. Moore. I trust you're Oak-kay. Even worse.

Hello, I couldn't be Moore excited to meet you. Hmmmm, this required some serious thought.

Finally, the studio rep led them towards a very special room. Ozzy's heart fluttered in his chest when he saw his own name printed on a card and attached to the door. OZZY TATE. He had his own changing room! This was amazing! Ozzy and Becky checked out the dressing room: wine, beer, champagne, fruit, nuts, chocolate, tea, coffee. There was a shower and a toilet, as well as a number of bathroom facilities that Ozzy had never come across in his life.

Ozzy knew that London would be a little more expensive than the north of England. He turned to the rep. "How much does a cup of coffee cost?"

"Tea and coffee is free."

Ozzy nodded. "And how much is beer?"

"Beer and wine is free. Everything in here is free."

Ozzy nodded. "And how much is—"

"Everything in this room is free. Please help yourself." The rep pouted for a split second and then delivered his parting speech. "Hair and make-up will be along in about 20 minutes. You can wear your own clothes…" The guide's eyes silently addressed Ozzy's attire from head to foot. "Don't worry, we'll provide something for you. Have fun and break a leg!"

Becky poured herself a glass of wine and offered one to Ozzy, but he said that he wanted a clear head before meeting Oakland. On second thought, he wanted to be relaxed and confident, so he grabbed a beer. The beer tasted great; it was free. Ozzy sat and pondered for a moment. This time yesterday, he'd been flirting with a couple of local tarts in The French Horn. Twenty-four hours later, he'd saved another human's life, been on nineteen different TV channels, including *Russia Today* and *Al-Jazeera,* and was now in a London television studio, drinking free beer and nibbling free Brazil nuts, about to meet a random selection of celebrities including his boyhood hero, Kin Lej.

After a limp-wristed knock at the door, Allin MacRear burst into the room with his whitened teeth on show. Immediately, Ozzy subconsciously closed his mouth, feeling the stains grow on his teeth as he gaped in awe at TV presenter's dentures.

"Good evening," smiled MacRear, shaking Ozzy's hand vigorously. "I am so pleased to meet you, Mr Tate! You are a real-life hero. What you did last night with your toe was simply incredible. Incredible! I have these celebrities come in and whinge because they've had to take a twelve-hour flight to get here, and I sometimes wonder what the world is coming to. But then I hear stories like yours, and it makes me feel glad to be alive."

Ozzy had never really been a fan of Allin MacRear. However, he felt MacRear's warm, genuine affection coming across straight away.

"Now," MacRear continued, "makeup will be in soon so, before they get here, let's quickly talk about you. I need a few things that I can ask you about during the show."

"Okay," Ozzy smiled, "what do you want to know?"

"Tell me some stories about your toe."

Day 2: March 23 - Sunday Night

Two hours later, Ozzy had shared a number of toe tales with MacRear, been given a smart suit to wear, and had undergone the surgical application of make-up and hairspray. Nervously, he now stood outside the Green Room where the guests were penned in before they appeared on camera. He listened at the door. He could hear confident people chatting and laughing: Viola Vixen, Stephen Meadow, and Oakland Moore. Luckily, he'd drunk four free beers and a small glass of free wine, so he had a little Dutch courage. He took a deep breath and then went for it. Swinging the door open, he entered the cozy room. First he saw Stephen Meadow, the comedian and actor. Meadow stood up. Stephen Meadow from the TV. He was rather thin and just looked like a normal bloke. Even though he was Stephen Meadow from TV, he was just a normal human man.

Meadow spoke first, holding out his hand. "Hi, I'm Stephen. Nice to meet you. I saw you on the news. Brilliant foot work there! I'd say you're a *shoe-in* for a knighthood or something."

Ozzy shook his hand without saying anything. He was Stephen Meadow from the TV, and he was making jokes about Ozzy's foot already. Amazing! Next, he turned to see Viola Vixen. *I have masturbated over you so many times,* Ozzy thought to himself. Right now, she had wild, purple hair. As she leaned over the small coffee table that was in the center of the room, Ozzy got a clear and vivid picture of the former model's wonderful cleavage. She gave Ozzy a kiss on each cheek. Only in his most private, intimate moments alone did Ozzy Tate ever think that he'd get a close-up of Viola Vixen's cleavage and then receive a kiss.

"I'm Viola," she smiled. "Nice to meet you."

Her beautiful eyes seemed to have put Ozzy into a trance. "Mmmm…. Nice!" In order to return to his senses, Ozzy blinked a huge blink. Had he really just said "nice" to Viola Vixen? Idiot!

Finally, he turned to meet the final guest in the Green Room. When Oakland Moore stood up, he towered over Ozzy. He was a mountain of a man. He held out his enormous gorilla hand for Ozzy to shake. He was actually touching Oakland Moore. The actor, with his suave gray hair, had a deep voice and spoke with a Chicago accent. "The guys have just been telling me that you saved somebody's life today. That's some going!"

Ozzy throat was breadstick dry once again. At last, he managed to form an actual sentence for the first time in the green room. "Well," he stuttered, "saving one life at a time, I say, just like Kin Lej."

Oakland stared straight into Ozzy's eyes. Ozzy immediately regretted his geeky joke. Why had he said such a stupid thing? Oakland Moore was probably fed up with jokes about *Star Cry*. It had been more than twenty years since they made the damn films. Of course, he wouldn't find it funny. I bet Stephen Meadow hadn't made a joke about *Star Cry;* he'd probably said something witty or something topical about Oakland's new film. Ozzy didn't even know what Oakland's new film was called!

Suddenly, Oakland burst out laughing. It was a deep, infectious laugh that boomed its way into your soul. Viola Vixen and Stephen Meadow joined in laughing, too.

"You're a funny guy!" stated Oakland. "Make sure you use that line on the show. I'll definitely laugh. Here, grab yourself a beer."

What a bloody nice man! Oakland oozed confidence, and this appeared to convey itself onto Ozzy. Ozzy sat down next to his hero—the real Kin Lej!—and cracked open another can of beer. He felt at home with the group of celebrities.

By the time Ozzy was called to be interviewed in front of the television cameras, he was feeling buoyant and ready to entertain. Before he was called to the set, he darted back to his changing room, ripped off the shirt that they had provided for him and put on his navy *Star Cry* T-shirt. It would go down a storm!

As Ozzy waited by the side of the set, he became nervous. What if he couldn't speak properly? He'd always been able to speak, but now that he was by the side of the set, he couldn't remember any of the toe stories that he'd shared with MacRear. He couldn't even remember any of the words that he'd said to him. He'd even forgot who the other celebrities were. He knew Oakland, of course, but who were the others? His palms started to sweat. Why had he decided to put the *Star Cry* T-shirt on? He looked an idiot; everyone would think so. Then he heard his name announced. This was it: time to be on TV. He began walking towards the studio sofa. Was he even walking properly? He probably looked stupid. Although Ozzy was greeted on the set by a huge cheer from the studio audience, it did nothing to help with his confidence. He took his place on the studio sofa alongside his new celebrity friends, who had already been interviewed. The studio lights were boiling hot as they burned down on his face. Ozzy felt himself sweating immediately. He couldn't see the audience properly; they were just ghostlike outlines. Shadows. Watching and waiting for Ozzy to speak. His throat was suddenly dry again. He looked once more at the studio audience. Where was Becky? He couldn't see her. Just the shadows, waiting for Ozzy to start talking gibberish and make himself look like a fool.

MacRear, as camply as ever, took notice of Ozzy's T-shirt. "Star Cry?"

"I'm…" How could Ozzy make this funny? "I'm… a big fan." That wasn't funny.

There was, however, a titter from the audience.

Oakland Moore, noticing how nervous Ozzy was, decided to join in with his booming voice. "That's my guy!" He held out his palm for Ozzy to high-five. The audience were really laughing now. Ozzy felt his shoulders grow. He slapped palms with Oakland.

"So," it was MacRear talking again, "you saved somebody's life last night." The audience started cheering and whooping. "How did that feel?"

The studio lights didn't quite feel so hot any longer. Ozzy sat up straight before he spoke. "I thought to myself: what would Kin Lej do?" The studio audience loved it. There were cackles and hoots from each corner of the room. Oakland Moore moved in for another high five. *This is brilliant,* thought Ozzy. He had high-fived Oakland Moore twice on national television, and he was making people laugh…on national television!

The eccentric host sharply turned to Viola Vixen. "I remember when you were a hero, Viola…which century was that again?" The audience was in rapture now, howling with laughter. Viola Vixen giggled along too, just pleased to be given this shorthanded piece of the limelight.

MacRear continued asking him about the tale of his courageousness, causing more whooping and positive hollering from the crowd. Then, the kooky presenter urged Ozzy to reveal "The Star of the Show"…his toe. He did so with joy.

"Oh my goodness!" said Oakland Moore. "I haven't seen anything like that since we were on the set of *Star Cry!*" Everyone howled with laughter. Ozzy was a Cheshire Cat. Kin Lej had just cracked a joke about his toe! And the joke involved his favorite movie!

Moments later, MacRear revealed a number of humorous photos on the big screen that had been sent in by Ozzy's family members.

Ozzy holding a baby with his toe.

Ozzy eating an ice cream with his toe.

Ozzy using his toe to fill his car with petrol.

"So, what other tricks can you do with your toe then?" asked the MacRear, sounding far more camp than he had done in Ozzy's changing room.

"I say, I can hammer nails into the wall. I can put on my tie."

Before he knew it, MacRear had brought out a tie, and Ozzy was using his feet to fasten it around Oakland Moore's collar. He actually had his feet on the shoulders of Kin Lej. It was bizarre. It was surreal. It was beautiful. Soon, Ozzy was cracking big jokes and engaging gleefully in lyrical wordplay with MacRear.

After they'd finished filming, Ozzy's head felt like it was in a cozy, warm bubble. Becky greeted him at his changing room with a passionate kiss. He was the king of the world! Oakland Moore had disappeared without saying goodbye, but that didn't matter; Ozzy still felt happier than he ever had done in his life. First, he was a hero, now he was an entertainer, and there was a chance that he could work things out with Becky. The journey back to their hotel was a hazy blur. However, with Ozzy and Becky sharing a bed, what happened next was inevitable.

Day 3: March 24- Monday

Thge next morning, Ozzy checked his Twitter account again to discover that #supertoe was still trending worldwide.

Matthew @djmattywires

OMG @bigtoeOzzy The toe has just been around @ oaklandmooreofficial's neck! #supertoe #legends

Kalindi @kalindi_

@bigtoeOzzy and his toe are hilarious! #supertoe

Sei-Ting @sei-ting

@bigtoeOzzy and @oaklandmooreofficial having pure banter with the toe on @prattlebattle #supertoe

List Hero @list_hero

@oaklandmooreofficial and @bigtoeOzzy should make a movie together about that toe! #supertoe

Da Kat @tippythecat11

@bigtoeOzzy when is you toe coming Indonesia? #supertoe

Ozzy couldn't believe what was actually happening to him: a worldwide sensation, a lifesaver and, now, a TV personality. Things were beginning to look rosy with Becky, too. She awoke to see him gawping at his mobile phone.

"What are you looking at?" she smiled.

"I say, I can't believe how many messages I've had on Twitter! I've actually got more followers than Viola Vixen now!"

Becky croaked an early morning chuckle. "Shut up!"

"Honestly! People in Papua New Guinea want to see my toe! I didn't even know they had Twitter in Africa!"

Becky shook her head. "Papua New Guinea is near Australia, you tool!" She looked at her watch on the bedside table. "We need to get ready."

"Why?" Ozzy's eyes took in the beautiful sight of Becky's bare back.

"We've got a busy schedule today. TV and radio are all over you, and they're all paying, too!"

Before noon, Ozzy had been on six different radio stations and made two appearances on daytime television. Each time, he gleefully expressed how excited he'd been to meet his hero, Oakland Moore. In the afternoon, he was pushed in front of TV cameras three more times and was forced to repeat the Time stories on the radio five more times. It became monotonous. Ozzy became weary that the tales of his toe were drying up, and he became bored of hearing the sound of his own voice. Dragged from studio to studio, Ozzy's toe was still hailed as the hero of the year. By the time Ozzy arrived for his final interview of the day, *Perry Gordon's Big Questions,* he felt blurry-eyed and drained of energy. He knocked back an extremely strong coffee, but it appeared to have little effect on his heavy head.

Perry Gordon had a reputation as a tearjerker. He would get to the heart of someone's past and bring out their deepest emotions. Due to the style of the presenter's questioning, *Perry Gordon's Big Questions* always appeared as though the guests were being grilled by a lawyer at the crown court. Ozzy prepared himself. He knew what was coming: missing the death and funeral of his grandma because he'd been working in Australia for a year. He'd probably bring up his breakup with Becky, too. Ozzy felt that this could actually work in his favor; a few tears over her, and she'd see how much she meant to him. He just needed to pick up his energy levels so that he could focus on saying the right things.

Becky could see that Ozzy was feeling below par. "Are you okay?" she asked with genuine concern.

"Just tired. Promise me that we don't have to go on any shows tomorrow."

Becky smiled and gave him a whole-hearted hug. "I promise."

"Let's just spend the day in bed," Ozzy suggested, "together."

Now Becky had a sparkle in her eye. "Okay." She kissed him. "I love you."

Ozzy's heart did a triple somersault and a double pike. "I love you, too. I'm sorry that I didn't try harder. Does this mean you're willing to give us another chance?"

Becky gave him a cheeky smile, and before she had the chance to say anything, Ozzy's name was announced for his arrival on the set.

Becky pushed him towards the stage and wandered off to find her seat in the audience.

After the announcement of his name, Ozzy entered the studio to the applause from the audience that he'd become accustomed to. He felt that the cheers had become gradually less enthusiastic since his appearance on the *Prattle Battle*. Or maybe he was just getting used to the noise of the audience, and it no longer surprised him as much. Either way, the atmosphere on this particular set was different to the others. There was an element of tension in the air.

Ozzy observed his interviewer, Perry Gordon. His face had an element of smugness to it; his closed-mouth smile seemed to tuck under his eyelids as his chin stretched to his chest. The presenter's eyes resembled those of a cat that has just come across a wounded blackbird. *You're in trouble now,* they seemed to be saying. *There's no escape.* Ozzy took in Gordon's Rolex watch and his thousand-pound suit. Gordon welcomed him onto the set with a sly wink. Ozzy felt uncomfortable from the moment he sat down.

"Oslo Percy Tate, you were born in Swegwood General Hospital and have spent your whole life living there. Is that correct?"

"Well, yes, apart from when I went to Australia for a year."

"Is it true that you have size 19 feet?" There was a titter from the audience.

"It is indeed."

"And is this uncommon shoe size mainly due to an extremely large toe?" A faint cheer from the audience followed this question.

"Not mainly due to the toe. I say, I'm half foot, half toe." This was received with a giggle.

"On March 22nd of this year, is it true that you used your extensive shoe size to save the life of Robert Lowe, who had fallen from a bridge in your home town of Skegwood?" At this question, the entire studio audience got to their feet and applauded for a good two minutes.

Once they had all sat down, Ozzy confirmed that it was true.

"And is it true," Gordon continued, "that you were investigated by the police for sexually abusing your younger brother Joshua during your teenage years?"

A feeling of nausea engulfed Ozzy's entire body. His stomach vibrated, and he felt the commencement of vomit approaching his throat. Where on earth had this question come from? Was it even legal to ask this on television? Did Ozzy need a lawyer? He couldn't focus on the man asking the questions any longer. He felt dizzy and overheated.

Ozzy's dry voice eventually simpered an answer. "Ye—"

This story was something that Ozzy had locked away in the deepest chamber of his mind's mazy castle. When he was eighteen years old, his brother Joshua was thirteen. Joshua was gay. He'd always known and so had his family. When Joshua hit his teenage years, he felt confident enough to tell the whole world. While uncles and grandparents felt that he was a little young to be making such announcements, Joshua's immediate family understood, and Ozzy didn't care; Joshua was Joshua, gay or not. The kids at school were not so understanding. Joshua didn't mind. They had called him a "filthy faggot" before he came out so it was irrelevant to him. For Ozzy, however, it hadn't been such a smooth ride. The rumor-mill worked overtime, and terrible lies were soon being churned out at a rapid pace. However, there was one disgusting story that seemed to stick. Teenage reasoning concluded that Joshua was gay because Ozzy had been abusing him throughout their childhood. Most adolescents, struggling with their hormonal balance, found it hilarious to think that someone they knew had been inserting his long toe into his brother's anal passage.

Once a group of parents got wind of the story, their children's humor was converted into disgust and then anger, and then they reported the allegations to the police. Ozzy, his brother, and his parents were all interviewed about the issue, but it was quickly dropped by the police. The brothers took a week off school while the commotion died down and, while they were off, the head teacher warned the rest of the school that they must cease such repulsive chitchat immediately.

Ozzy finished school a few months later, and, along with his best friends, Matthew and Tez, decided to get away from Skegwood for a year. Their parents bought them tickets to Australia, and the three friends spent the year working, partying, and growing up together down under.

"But that wasn't true, of course?" Gordon's voice startled Ozzy back into the room.

"No. Horrible lies. Teenagers, you know."

"It must have been terrible in school?"

"I'd rather forget about that."

Gordon nodded with his eyes closed. "Of course. So, is that why you fled to Australia for a year after you finished school?"

"I guess so."

"And, through all of those difficult times, your girlfriend at the time, Becky, stood by you. Is that right?"

"Of course, she did. She knew that it was all lies."

"And yet," Gordon's eyes were predatory cat once again, "despite her loyalty to you, you couldn't return the favor. I have been informed by a reliable source that, during your time in Australia, you experimented with a number of different drugs. When you went out, you preferred cocaine. When you stayed in, you enjoyed ketamine. Is this true?"

Ozzy's lips felt like they were cracking on air. His once-smooth forehead was now corduroy with worry. "Where did you hear this?"

Gordon ignored his question. "Jennifer Kite, Michelle Mitchell, Sarah Coleman, Bo Min, and Meena Chaudhury all claim that they had sex with you in Australia while you were supposed to be in a committed relationship with Becky. Is this true?"

It was. Ozzy had been weak in Australia. He'd been a drunk and by the time he'd smashed through a box of goon, a nasty wine that was cheap enough for the poorly paid boys to drink at barbecues, his inhibitions were a distant speck on the horizon. Rational decision making was not at the top of drunken Ozzy's priorities. The goon encouraged him to grab at Eden's apple and led him down the path of dishonesty. His closest three friends had managed to keep this all to themselves, and nobody outside of that group knew about any of it…until now.

"Is this true?" repeated Gordon like a formidable lawyer pushing for a guilty verdict in a murder trial.

"I don't know," replied Ozzy, flustered.

"You don't know if you had sex with Jennifer Kite, Michelle Mitchell, Sarah Coleman, Bo Min, and Meena Chaudhury? They have all contacted this program and claimed that it's the truth. Maybe the air miles have effected your memory. Okay, let's try this one. Lilly O'Patrick. She lives in Skegwood, just like you."

Ozzy's heart played an irregular beats on his ribs. Becky knew Lily O'Patrick. His eyes searched the audience, but he couldn't see her, just rows and rows of disdainful looks, all wishing that they'd never laid eyes on Ozzy Tate and his filthy, unfaithful ways.

The presenter went on. "Lily O'Patrick claims that you had an on-going relationship behind Becky's back. She claims that there was drink and drugs, and she even snorted cocaine off your toe." The audience groaned in disgust. "She said that you had sex numerous times in the bed that was meant to be shared by only you and Becky." This time there was a gasp of revolted amazement. "Is this true?"

Ozzy didn't want to be on TV anymore. The excitement of being a minor celebrity had all but disintegrated. Meeting Oakland Moore felt like a dream, something that happened in a past life, a distant memory. He just wanted to be with Becky, to explain what had happened with Lily O'Patrick. To tell her that it was all a silly mistake. To calm her down, talk her around. He wanted Becky to say it was okay. He'd only just won her back. He didn't want to lose her again so quickly.

The rest of the interview was a blur. Ozzy couldn't focus on his answers properly. When the recording ended, there was a scattering of polite claps but the majority of people were too shocked at the evening's revelations to do anything.

Ozzy immediately grabbed his phone and tried to call Becky. No answer. He searched the studio and went to his changing room. She was nowhere to be seen, and nobody had noticed her leave.

Day 4: March 25 – Tuesday afternoon

After failing to find or get in touch with Becky throughout the whole night, Ozzy was forced to return to the north of England by public transport: the two changes on the London underground, one train up north, and the local bus to Skegwood felt like a grueling test of his mental strength. Firstly, he'd been jeered at by a group of youths on the underground. Then, on the train, a woman called him a "cheating pig" and spat in his overpriced cup of coffee before she got off. And finally, on the bus back to Skegwood, Ozzy chose the sweetest old lady to sit next to, assuming that she hadn't watched *Perry Gordon's Big Questions*. She had. She immediately stood up, called him a "dirty cunt," and went to sit on a different seat.

Ozzy couldn't really understand the full extent of the animosity toward him. Didn't everyone dabble in a bit of narcotics these days? And men and women everywhere seemed to be playing away at some point, too.

However, as Ozzy browsed the Internet on his phone, the hatred soon became clear to him. Once Ozzy had become public enemy number one, the rumor mill had gone into overdrive. Under the pseudonym of "news," fictional stories were popping up all over the place about Ozzy's shady past. Apparently, he had links to Al-Qaeda, was a big player in the blood diamond market, and had a history of animal torture. Someone had claimed he scratched the car of a war veteran, another said he'd got a fifteen-year-old schoolgirl hooked on heroin, and others stated that he'd sold them cakes, pretending that the proceeds went to a charity that didn't exist.

Looking at his Twitter account brought him no further joy. He was called a toe rapist; a dirty, lying, big-toed cunt; a cheating druggy prick, and a paed-toe-phile. People sent him messages describing the ungodly acts that they'd like to perform on him: sticking his own toe up his ass; cutting off his cock and toe and then blending them in a soup for Ozzy to eat; inventing a toe-stubbing machine so that it happened to him all day; strapping explosives to his toe and sending it to Pakistan. The list went on.

At every stage of Ozzy's journey home, he felt vicious eyes burning their glares through his soul, hours and hours of mental torture with vile, paranoid thoughts thrashing inside his head like a steroid-injected wasp of revulsion. His feet had begun to ache, too; a burning sensation had started to throb in his big toes, like they'd been aggressively rubbed with a freshly chopped chili. It was the most uncomfortable journey of Ozzy's life, both mentally and physically.

When he eventually arrived back home, Ozzy had never felt so relieved to slam the door behind him, shutting out the world of gossip and hatred. He instantly ripped off his shoes to try to cool down his burning, aching toes. With Matthew back at work, the flat was empty. The events of the past few days, and particularly the previous evening, finally caught up with Ozzy; he curled up in a ball on the floor and wept into the carpet for thirty minutes straight.

By the time that he'd eventually pulled himself together, Ozzy was angry. Angry with the boy that fell off the bridge. If he hadn't fallen, Ozzy's toe wouldn't have saved him, Becky wouldn't have called, and then his darkest, dirtiest laundry wouldn't have been aired in public. Robert Lowe was his name. The cunt. If he hadn't fallen so far down the bridge, Matt could have reached him and Ozzy's toe wouldn't have been needed. Ozzy's fucking toe! Why did it have to be so fucking long? Let's face it, people were no more interested in Ozzy than they were a blade of grass. It was the toe that they wanted—they craved. All just part of life's never-ending freak show: the elephant man, the bearded lady, the gigantic, fucked-up toe. The toe that people snort cocaine off, the toe that rapes young boys, the toe that people on the Internet were calling to be carved off and blended into a hearty soup.

Ozzy was eventually startled from his thoughts by a shooting pain in his foot. Ozzy's toes were really beginning to itch now. They felt sore.

As Ozzy felt a rumble in his tummy, he realized that he hadn't eaten since he feasted on free Brazil nuts in Perry Gordon's Green Room the previous evening. He pulled himself away from the tear-soaked carpet and grabbed the pineapple that was sitting alone in his otherwise empty fruit bowl. With tears still escaping his eyes and nose, he drew his sharpest knife from his top drawer and began to slice the rough skin away from the fruit.

Once a few chunks of juicy pineapple had quenched both his hunger and thirst, he grabbed his trusty bottle of Southern Comfort and poured himself a pint—a pint without a mixer, solely liquor. With three great swags, Ozzy dragged the drink down his towards his belly. The strong liquor warmed his throat, and the drink's sweet flavors allowed him to gulp the whole pint. Ozzy immediately felt a hazy glow take over his body; his head felt loose. He poured himself a second pint of Southern Comfort and flopped onto the sofa.

In just four days, Ozzy had been to the peak of his life's emotional mountain. They say that everybody gets their fifteen minutes of fame. But…four days? It hadn't even felt like four minutes! And they say that what goes up must inevitably come down. Boy, had Ozzy come down, no longer able to leave the house or look his family in the eye. They had loved Becky like a daughter, and he had betrayed her. Becky's family had loved him, too, but now they, as well as the entire world, knew about his devious ways. And what was the cause of Ozzy's fatal plummet towards the Earth? His freaky fucking toe, an apparently hideous, raping toe. Ozzy pulled off his socks to take a look at his toes. He despised them. He wanted to rip off the toenails. Bite off the toes with his teeth. Ozzy heard himself growl like a wild beast.

He went to the bathroom to take a piss. He wanted to wipe his dick afterward but the toilet roll holder was empty. *Wankers!* He wanted to wash his hands, too, but the liquid soap dispenser was also empty. *Cunts!* Ozzy's right fist thrashed into the mirror in frustration, cracking it instantly, and cutting up his knuckles with its broken shards. Ozzy enjoyed the pain. It felt nice. He dug one of his left fingernails into the deepest of the cuts. It was joyously painful. He pressed as far as he could go. Ozzy's nervous system went into overdrive with pleasurable agony.

He glugged back half of his second liquor pint. This time, it hurt a little more. He clenched his teeth, growling again, and then jumped to his feet. He needed a plan. He needed a cure. What had harmed him? What had caused this? The only route to saving his life must surely be to tackle the cause of his issues. Find the cure, destroy the cause.

Ozzy stomped around his living room, poking his cut knuckles, sending messages of pain to his brain. He went back and forth like a demented tiger at a rundown zoo whose enclosure was far too small. His eyes were wide and wild. He marched into the kitchen. Out of the corner of his eye, Ozzy spotted the sharp knife that he'd used to carve up his pineapple. He grabbed it with both hands, like a samurai holding his precious sword, and inspected it from tip to handle. Find the cure, destroy the cause.

Ozzy was excited now. The predator had found its prey. His eyes glazed over. Find the cure, destroy the cause. He rushed into the lounge and positioned himself carefully on the sofa. Destroy the cause. Ozzy enjoyed the pain.

Day 4: March 25 – Tuesday evening

Sitting behind the wheel of his van, Matthew sucked in some well-deserved nicotine as he made his way home for the evening. His day had been unnecessarily stressful as he attempted to improve the water facilities for Skegwood's ungrateful citizens. Despite their lack of training, most of the idiots seemed to think that they knew better than the plumber that had been assigned to supply running water to their flea-pit tenancies. The unemployed, which 99 percent of the tenants were, had no interest in taking Matthew's advice, and, quite frankly, it frustrated him to the back teeth.

Blowing smoke out of his open window, Matthew felt dread take over his body when it dawned upon him that it was only Tuesday; it felt like Thursday, at least. The first two days of this eventful week seemed to have lasted an eternity. But it wasn't just the work that seemed to have stretched the week out; so much had happened since Saturday. Seeing one of your closest companions on television all week had been simply surreal. Ever since his best friend, Ozzy Tate, had become an overnight celebrity, people had been getting in touch from all over the place. It was manic!

Last night's episode of *Big Questions*, however, had been difficult viewing. Matthew hadn't liked seeing all of Ozzy's dark secrets made public, especially since he—Matthew—had known about them all along. Hell, he'd even encouraged Ozzy's mischief on a few occasions. Boys will be boys, while the cat's away, and whatever else it is that temptation tells us. For Becky to find out about Ozzy's wrongdoings would have been one thing, but for the entire world to know must have been soul shattering for Ozzy. Matthew knew that his best friend was thick-skinned because of what had happened with the school rumors. This, however, was a different level of scandal. And it had been thrust upon him in a harsh, unexpected manner.

Matthew was seriously concerned about his friend. He'd called and texted and sent him a message on Facebook, but Ozzy had made no response. Matthew had even tried to ring Becky, but, as he expected, she didn't answer.

As he parked his Citroen Berlingo on the street outside their shared flat, Matthew wondered if he'd find Ozzy inside. He finished off his cigarette, stamped it into the pavement, and walked toward his front door. Unlike when he left the house, the curtains were now closed. Ozzy was home. Matthew imagined the scene; Ozzy wrapped up in a duvet on the sofa, blood-shot eyes, surrounded with beer cans and *Star Cry 2* on the big screen TV. Ozzy always watched *Star Cry 2* when he was feeling blue; there were hundreds of mistakes in the movie, and it made Ozzy angry, which somehow drew him out of depression. Matthew didn't really understand, but Ozzy always seemed to feel better afterward.

Matthew carefully opened the flat door. His heart fell to his feet. Not in a million years could he have anticipated what he saw when he peered into the darkened flat. He immediately turned back into the fading sunlight of the March evening and splashed projectile vomit into the street. Matthew froze, staring away from the door. He couldn't turn around. He feared facing the dreadful sight once more.

✕◐✕ ✕◐✕ ✕◐✕ ✕

About the Author

Daniel Henshaw is a qualified primary school teacher and holds a degree in English Studies. Well, he held it once; they took a photo of him wearing a silly hat, and he's never seen it since. When Daniel's not shouting at children, he writes stories for them instead (as well as short fiction for adults). His tales have been published by magazines such as *Scholars & Rogues* and *Story Shack*. Daniel likes dogs and liquorice (though usually not at the same time).

ONE FOR SORROW

J.D. Kotzman

In folklore, crows often serve as harbingers of doom and death, probably something to do with their dusky plumage, eerie calls, and unnerving penchant for carrion. They also tend to congregate in macabre places—battlefields, murder scenes, and the like. A *murder*, that's what they call a flock of crows. Apart from their morbid symbolism, though, there's a quaint tradition, some centuries-old, of counting crows as a kind of augury, a way of divining the future based on the number of them present at significant times. As a girl, growing up on my father's farm, I liked to count the crows, sometimes even chanting a version of the catchy little nursery rhyme that goes along with the practice. I suppose I stopped believing in that sort of whimsy when I got older and learned a thing or two about life. But looking back, maybe I shouldn't have. Maybe I should have paid more attention to the crows, kept better tally. If I close my eyes and think hard, I can almost picture them gathered on the fat, withered elm outside our aged farmhouse—three (for a wedding) on the morning Roy and I got hitched, four (for a birth) on the afternoon Jonny burst into the world, and years later, eight (for dying) on the evening my husband overturned his beloved John Deere into a ditch.

A few months after the accident, when the bank foreclosed, I left the farm behind for good and settled into a small place in town. As for the prophetic birds, they followed me. They never wavered from their duty. Just before that bastard boy first darkened my door, I can recall, with near-perfect clarity, peering out the window and spying, atop a crooked telephone pole, a single crow (for sorrow), its piercing, urgent cries calling to me, as if in warning.

XOXOX

"Who's the new inmate?" I heard someone, a man, ask. "Jesus, he's fucked up."

"Goodman, Jonathan R.—attempted suicide, took a header off a ridge or something," another man said. Something padded tightened around my each of my wrists, then my ankles. "Came in last night. He's on the good shit; high as a goddamn kite. Doubt we even need these. He hasn't so much as twitched since my shift started."

"What's with 5-O outside?"

"He's wanted for questioning. Killed someone, they say."

"Damn. For real? He looks like he's just a kid."

"Yeah, no joke."

"Hey, can he hear us?"

"Nah, I don't think so," the first man said, cackling. "I'd wager that fall squashed his melon but good."

I pulled my Ford to a stop by the side of an unmarked, long-forgotten access road, slipped out of the oversized cab, and unloaded our things from the truck bed. At the edge of the gravel path, where the coarse pebbles gave way to lush earth, Wendy and I steeled ourselves for the grisly task ahead. We took a careful last look for any stray passersby, and then, seeing none, began our trek into the seemingly never-ending rows of corn. Under the slate-gray autumn sky, the air felt heavy, stock-still, but as we cut deeper into the field, a chilly breeze kicked up. The gangly stalks bowed in deference, and, amid the branches of a nearby tree—an ancient, wiry oak that rose like an island from the sea of maize—a cluster of black birds cawed nervously. *Fucking crows.* My mother probably would have tried to count them, claimed the number meant something or other. I didn't have time for that nonsense, though, not then. A little later, when Wendy and I emerged in a small clearing, she squeezed my hand, and the two of us exchanged uneasy glances. *As good of a place as any*, I thought, nodding to her. I dropped the large burlap sack I'd dragged along with us, and for a while, we could only stare, in awe, at our strange, lifeless cargo.

"I should get started," I said, breaching the hush. "It'll be dark soon."

"Yeah, guess so," Wendy said, handing me the round-pointed spade she'd carried. As I clutched the steel handle, a tiny, ominous shudder ran through me. "Jonny, I'm scared."

"Come here," I said, lodging the shovel blade in the ground. When I took her in my arms, she pressed her soft cheek to my chest, and her silky blonde hair brushed the underside of my chin. "It's going to be all right."

"How can you say that?" she asked, pushing away from me, almost in tears. "How can things ever be all right after this?"

"I don't know," I growled, choking back the anger welling inside me.

"I'm sorry, Jonny."

"So am I."

I seized the spade from its resting place, plunged it deep into the soil, and cast aside a clump of loose sod. While I dug, I relived those final, horrible moments with Billy. I could see his twisted, ashen face, the sheer terror in his eyes as I stood over him, seething, my Louisville Slugger cocked menacingly. I could hear the thundering cracks of aluminum against bone, the shrieks of agony as I brought the bat down, again and again, until he lay motionless at my feet. And as I lingered around his battered body, the fury oozing out of me, I could feel the blood, his blood, still hot, spattered on my face, down my arms, through my sweat-soaked T-shirt. *Christ, so much blood...* CLANG! The loud jangle and subsequent jolt drowned my lurid vision in a wash of irritation and pain, and the shovel, which I'd managed to slam into a furtive chunk of rock, tumbled weakly to the ground.

"Goddammit."

"What's wrong?" Wendy asked, concern flooding her face.

"I'm fine," I said, retrieving the fallen spade. "Everything's going to be fine."

"I want to believe you; I do."

I offered her a wry smile and looked off into the distance. The sunset cast a blazing glow over the corn, and along the horizon, the yellowing stalks flared bright orange, as if they'd caught fire. For a moment, I couldn't help but admire the beauty of it all.

"You know, we used to have cornfields like this one…back when my father was still around," I told her, my gaze stuck on the skyline. "As a kid, I used to play in them for hours—hide-and-seek, army, zombie apocalypse, whatever other lunatic games I could imagine. I never wanted to go home."

"What happened to him?"

"My father?" I asked, turning to face her again.

"Yes, you never told me."

"He died."

"Oh, Jonny…I'm sorry."

"Don't be," I said.

Only the incessant chirping of the crickets broke the uncomfortable, protracted quiet that followed between us.

After an hour of digging, I dropped the spade by my side and began wrestling with the hefty sackcloth bag, struggling to topple it into the shallow hole I'd excavated. I won the battle, but before I could relish the ensuing *THUNK*, a gentle stirring in the corn spooked me. With the incursion creeping ever closer, I snatched the shovel and ducked into the shadows, my weapon raised, poised to strike.

"Jonny? Jonny, where are you?"

"Wendy," I muttered, relieved. I stepped back into the moonlight, eager to see her seraphic face. "I was worried. Where have you been?"

"I checked the main road like you said, then stopped to get us some dinner," she explained, holding up a grease-spotted paper sack.

"Thanks, but I'm not hungry," I said. I hadn't eaten since breakfast, but the thought of food made my stomach recoil. "I need to finish this anyway."

Wendy sat down in the dirt and pried open her bag, and I observed for a bit as she absently munched on a handful of fries. At nineteen, only four years younger than me, the biggest part of her had stayed a child, a delicate quality I both cherished and envied. We met a few months ago at a dingy, cramped diner, where she spent many an hour hustling grub to some of the worst tippers imaginable—slimy drunks who'd squirmed out of the neighboring bar, tired young parents with their ill-behaved progeny in tow, raucous teenagers, and on Sundays, carloads of testy church-going geezers—all in the grand hope of collecting enough of their pocket change to pay for nursing school in the city. Anything to get out of her father's house and away from that miserable town, she confided later. By Wendy's account, her relationship with her dad began to sour about the time she turned fourteen, after her mother left them and shacked up with the starting shortstop for some Double-A club down south. Her father never really recovered from that, maybe even blamed her for it, she said, and by high school graduation, things between them had gotten so tense and knotty, she could hardly stand the sight of him. Yet, by my reckoning, she'd somehow remained unbroken.

But I didn't know any of those things about Wendy when I pushed through the chrome-and-glass door, climbed up onto an empty barstool, and propped my elbows on the weathered Formica countertop. I certainly didn't know she would change my life. I just knew that I'd spotted a pretty girl, wearing an inviting smile and an ugly but oddly alluring gum-colored uniform, and that I wanted to get close to her. So I grabbed her attention and ordered a coffee, and with a shy grin, she went off to fetch my drink. When she returned, I chanced a line, asking what a nice girl like her was doing in a place like that. Stupid and clichéd, I realized, but it worked. She giggled and asked my name. After an awkward introduction, we got to talking, carrying on a spasmodic, flirty conversation until her shift ended.

Much later that night, while Wendy and I lay together under the dull green light from my dashboard, she slid her fingers over the bandages encircling my wrist. When she broached the subject, I invented a flimsy lie—"a slip of a box cutter," I said—but in truth, without the farm, living didn't make sense to me anymore. I'd spent a couple of weeks slaving for minimum wage at the new discount superstore that opened in the next county, and even though the job more or less took care of the bills, it left me desperately craving the familiar rituals and rhythms of working the land, tending the animals.

My existence felt like an empty husk, and I hated it, hated myself. If I hadn't stumbled upon Wendy, I might have wound up bleeding out in my shabby bathtub or meeting some other equally pathetic end. She encouraged me to see beyond the long hours and bad pay, beyond the stark, white walls and harsh fluorescent lights, beyond the herds of pushy, dim-witted customers stampeding through the aisles each day. She showed me how to dream again. With her beside me, little by little, things got more bearable, even enjoyable. Enjoyable, at least, until Billy turned up and ruined everything.

"Jonny, I love you."

"I know," I said. "I love you too."

"Jonny," Wendy whispered, after a while. "How did your dad die?"

"Tractor accident," I told her, continuing to cover the makeshift grave with dirt. "At least, as far as anyone knows."

"What do you mean?"

"It's complicated," was all I said.

I kept working, but the talk of my father set my mind to unearthing some grim childhood memories, ones I'd hoped would stay dead and buried, just like him. The one that haunted me most happened when my mother went away, a few weeks before my thirteenth birthday, to visit her cancer-stricken sister. My dad had always frightened me, but maybe never quite so much as when he returned from the fields that evening, only the two of us in the house. Beads of sweat dotted his brow, and his imposing frame towered in the kitchen doorway, blotting out the setting sun. Once inside, he snagged a couple of cold cans of PBR from our rusty antique refrigerator, popped one open, then the second, and sat guzzling them at the table, waiting for me to serve him his reheated meatloaf and mashed potatoes. After we ate dinner, mostly in silence, he showered, changed, and drove his weatherworn Dodge pickup to the local roadside tavern. For my part, I cleaned the dishes, watched a little TV, and tried to get some sleep.

The telltale squeak of the front door jarred me awake sometime in the wee hours, and I lay quietly, trembling under the covers, praying for my father to pass out on the couch. He often did after a night at the bar. On that night, though, he came home angry, bent with rage. I'd forgotten to gas up his truck like he'd asked—why, exactly, I can't remember anymore—and he ended up having to foot the last half-mile, or thereabout. When he got back to the house, he lumbered up the creaky wooden stairs, staggered into my bedroom, and undid his belt. "Get up, boy, you lazy sonofabitch," he roared, eyes wild, breath reeking of cheap whisky and Marlboros. What happened next, not for the first or last time, I longed to forget. But the thwacks of leather against my skin, over and over, still echoed in my head, long after the pain had subsided and the nasty, persistent welts had faded. I wept afterward, but he didn't see the tears. I didn't let him. *Fuck him... and fuck his bastard son too.* Until a week ago, I never even knew Billy existed. And as I heaped the last of the earth over him, I found myself wishing, maybe more than anything, that he hadn't.

"Why did you do it?" Wendy asked softly, her eyes filling with tears as we hovered above the fresh tomb. "He was your own brother."

"Half-brother," I corrected, but her expression remained fraught with disbelief. "It's probably best you didn't know."

"Tell me. Please, tell me."

"Okay," I conceded, figuring I owed her at least that, and much more besides. "My father didn't die by accident. He made it look like an accident, so my mother could collect on his life insurance policy and try to save the farm. It was the only decent thing he ever did, at least the only one I can remember."

"Your dad killed himself?"

"Yes," I said, taking her hand. We trudged through the corn, guided only by the dim light of the moon. "Anyway, Billy, my half-brother, showed up at my mother's apartment last week. He wanted money—money she didn't have, what with the investigation still ongoing. If she didn't give it to him, he said he'd turn her in for insurance fraud, claimed he had some papers from my father to prove it."

"So you had no choice."

"We all have a choice," I said. "He made his, and I made mine."

A radio squawked in the direction of the road. My head jerked toward the disturbance, and I caught sight of red and blue lights pulsing against the inky sky. I wrapped an arm around Wendy, and we crouched down amid the corn, neither of us daring to utter a word. The sheriff, Sam Coldwell—good ol' Sammy Lawman, my father used to call him, back in their drinking days—had come for me. He barked out some orders, and after rumbling their agreement, his deputies fanned out into the field, their 12-gauges locked and loaded. While they canvassed the area, we stayed hunkered, our faces concealed from the nosy flashlight beams that kept poking through the stalks. Sometime later, the sheriff himself plodded into the cornfield and stopped only a few feet from our snug huddle, imploring us to surrender. I put a hand to Wendy's mouth and held my breath, anticipating our imminent capture, but Coldwell veered off along a different trajectory. When he'd gone, I noticed her trembling, whimpering and gripped her tighter. Hunger suddenly hit me. My shoulders hurt, and everything else ached, racked with exhaustion. We couldn't hold out there much longer, I knew, and I needed to get Wendy clear of me, of all of it. So, when I sensed an opening, I ran.

I bolted through the tangle of stalks, careening toward a swath of trees that bordered the far side of the field. The blades of corn scraped my arms and face as I plowed through them, and a firebomb detonated in my chest, my heart and lungs rebelling against me. Behind me, over the sounds of my labored breathing and the rustling maize, I heard a cacophony of voices, all ordering me to stop, give myself up. I sprinted harder, though, and even Wendy's plaintive cries as the officers pounced on her didn't slow me. Finally free of the cornfield, I darted into the wooded patch, hurtling though the timber and down a muddy slope that led to a deep ravine. A warning blast from a shotgun rang out, shaking me, but I kept my feet, kept going. As I neared the gorge, I stopped short and wheeled around to face my pursuers, watching as they crested the hill and charged toward me, their torches alight, like a crazed, angry mob. I had nowhere to run, nowhere to hide. I turned back toward the waiting chasm, rushed to the edge, and leapt headlong into the darkness below.

"Is he dead?" someone yelled. I heard approaching footfalls, grunts, wheezing. Clammy fingers pressed against my neck.

"He has a pulse. Radio for an ambulance," someone else said, just before everything went dark.

"I need to ask him some questions."

"He's still under heavy sedation," a man, a doctor, said as he shined a light into my eyes. "He won't be able to respond. Given the severity of his injuries, he might never be able to respond. It's too early to tell."

"Jonny! Jonny, can you hear me? I know you can hear me, you sonofabitch."

"If you come back later, when the medication has worn off, perhaps…"

"Goddamnit, boy, wake up!" shouted the other one, a man whose voice I recognized—*Dad…no, no, Coldwell.*

But their talk became distorted after that, and I ceased listening. I only stared blankly, with my one functioning eye, at the lone crow nested on the windowsill. One for sorrow, my mother told me once, ages ago. Already plunged in despair, my spirit sunk even lower, weighed down by the hard, simple truth of her words. Then a second black bird landed by the first. At the sight of it, my heart fluttered, and if my face still worked, I might have beamed. One for sorrow, she'd said, one for sorrow, and two for mirth.

About a month after Jonny passed, the long-awaited insurance check finally arrived in the mail. Blood money, money that cost me almost everything I loved, but money I needed, so I took it all the same. A week later, on a blustery afternoon I'd spent perched by my kitchen window, idly eying a pair of crows hopping along a telephone wire, I got an unexpected guest. I'd never met Wendy before then, but seeing her shivering on my front stoop—going on about my son, tears streaking down her flushed cheeks—melted my heart. I invited her inside for a mug of chamomile, and while we sat together at my second-hand colonial table, sipping hot tea and nibbling on slightly stale biscuits, she told me her story, how she met Jonny, helped him through a rough patch a while back. Later, when she'd screwed up enough courage, she recounted what happened in the cornfield that dreaded day, the last day my boy spoke to either of us. Afterward, the two of us shared a long hug and a good, soul-cleansing cry.

After that first visit, Wendy came back to see me a few more times and, eventually, moved into my spare bedroom. She needed someone to take care of her, I suspected. She told me her mother had skipped out years ago, and though she said her father had raised her as best he could, I got the sense he didn't have much use for a little girl, let alone a lovely young woman who constantly reminded him of his cheating ex-wife. As for me, I'd always wanted a daughter, and with Roy and Jonny gone, my life had grown rather lonely. I appreciated the newfound company.

So strange, it seems, the way things turned out. The crows knew, though. They'd always known, always tried to tell me, forewarn me, albeit in their own queer, cryptic fashion.

)O(O)( )O(O)( )O(O)( )(

About the Author

J.D. Kotzman works in the health policy field and lives in the Washington, D.C., area with his girlfriend and two pugs, Grendel and Ginger. Previously, he has served as an editor and writer for several print and online news publications. His fiction has appeared or is forthcoming in *The Bookends Review, The Chronos Chronicles* (a project of Indie Authors Press), *Crack the Spine, Drunk Monkeys, Foliate Oak, Inscape, Kentucky Review, Pidgeonholes, Slink Chunk Press, The Speculative Edge, Straylight, An Unlikely Companion* (a project of Spark), and *Yellow Chair Review.* Find more of his writing at amazon.com/author/jdkotzman.

YELLOW PILL

I. K. Paterson-Harkness

The wind blew hard, throwing the rain near to horizontal. Lata gripped her umbrella, facing away from the wind, and huffed into the thick scarf around her neck. The backs of her legs were soaked. A mother and her young son stepped out of the brightly lit pharmacy and ran across the empty car park. The boy wore bright orange gumboots and stomped through every puddle he came across, while his mother shrieked at him to leave the puddles alone. Eventually, the lights within the pharmacy went out, and Sarah emerged.

"Let's talk in the car!" she shouted and strode around the corner of the building toward the staff car park. Lata hurried after her, buffeted along by the wind.

"God, what a day," Sarah said, throwing her backpack onto the back seat. She inspected her reflection in the rear view mirror, undid her hair, then retied it into a messy bun. "At lunch, we had a line of people that stretched all the way to the door and half way back around the room. It's been absolute madness this week."

She pulled a plain white plastic bottle from her pocket and passed it to Lata. "I couldn't let the pharmacist see me give this to you, sorry. I told him I'd found the bottle on the shelf, and since it was unlabeled and he didn't recognize the pills, he sent some to the lab. He got—"

"He didn't recognize them?"

"No. He got a call from the lab this morning. Apparently, those pills have stumped everyone. But they're highly toxic: extremely high in potassium, chlorine, something else. How many is Joseph taking?"

"Eight a day."

"Oh my god! He should be seriously unwell."

"He even sets his alarm each night before we sleep so he can take one in the middle of the night. He takes one every few hours."

Sarah's eyes were wide and white in the dim light. "Lata, you need to talk to him. Those pills are poisonous. Where is he getting them from?"

Lata couldn't answer because she didn't know. Her stomach churned. The rain poured down the windscreen in hundreds of separate rivers, obscuring her view, the noise of it filling her mind. She opened the bottle and poured a few pills onto her hand. Other than the fact that they were banana yellow, they could have been aspirin.

"He says they're for his asthma," she said at last.

"They're not."

"Joseph? Oh. My. God!"

It had started last Saturday—Lata's suspicions that something wasn't quite right. She and Joseph had decided they'd try someplace new for breakfast and had just sat down at a table at the botanical garden's alfresco cafe when a slender, red-faced woman came suddenly running out at them from behind an overgrown rosemary bush.

"I can't believe it!" She panted, pulling up a chair for herself and collapsing into it. She was wearing running shoes and a loose-fitting gray hoodie. "I thought I saw you. When I was coming across the field. And I thought, 'Oh my god. Surely, it can't be?' But I'd know your strut anywhere. And look, here you are!"

Joseph blinked a few times at the smiling woman, then turned to Lata wide-eyed.

"Wow," he stammered at last. "Andrea, what a surprise! I mean, wow. It's been, what? Two, three years?"

"I know! I can't believe it! I've only been back in Auckland a fortnight, and I've bumped straight into you!"

"This is Lata. Lata, this is Andrea."

Lata knew exactly who she was. Andrea. The famous Andrea. Despite the fact that her face looked like a purple radish right now, she was undeniably beautiful and, quite frankly, that made Lata sick.

"It's nice to meet you," Andrea said, holding out a delicate hand.

Lata mumbled something in return, shook the hand, and then picked up the menu.

"What are you doing with yourself now, huh?" Andrea asked, leaning across the table on her elbows. "Are you still working at the tepid baths?"

Joseph's pocket began to beep. He pulled out his phone, turned the alarm off, and from the other pocket withdrew a bottle of pills. He shook one into his hand. Lata concentrated on the menu, reading the first line over and over. Home-made toasted muesli.

"Yeah, yeah. Same ol'," he said.

"Don't want to break the routine, do we?" She smiled like she'd just made some sort of personal joke.

Toasted muesli.

"Have you got in touch with your parents yet?"

"No."

"I've often wondered to myself whether you ever made amends."

"Still as estranged as ever."

She clicked her tongue. "What a shame. Are you guys married?" she asked, waggling her finger between Lata and Joseph.

"No," Lata said.

"I am," she said, holding out her left hand and displaying the golden ring. "Two years next month. And guess what?" She reached across the table and squeezed Joseph's arm. "I'm pregnant!" She did a small celebratory jiggle.

Well that was one good thing, Lata thought. The only reason Joseph and Andrea had broken up was because Andrea wanted babies, and Joseph couldn't provide them. Joseph had been very clear about that fact when he and Lata first started going out just over a year ago.

"I'm only just through the first trimester, but I can already feel Baby moving around inside me," Andrea said, patting her tummy. "We came back for Baby. I wanted to be close to Mum. She still asks about you, you know."

Joseph stood up. "Excuse me, but I need to get a drink of water. Lata, are you ready to order?"

"Just get me the muesli."

Without another word, Joseph walked off in the direction of the counter.

Andrea stretched her arms above her head, arching her back. "Well, I better keep going. I'm determined to stay fit throughout the pregnancy. It was nice to meet you, darl'." She gave a little wave, ran three steps, then turned on her heel. "You know, maybe this isn't my place," she said, "but I've discovered a great homeopath. She's apparently an expert at fixing skin problems."

Lata frowned and touched her face.

"Oh god, darl', not for you. Bless. You have the face of an angel. I mean for Joseph."

"Joseph?"

"I noticed he's still taking those awful pills."

"But they're for his asthma."

"They're for his skin. Joseph doesn't have asthma."

"I think I'd know."

Andrea pouted, her forehead crinkling, and Lata felt her cheeks grow hot. Andrea tipped her head to one side. "All I'm saying is that he's been taking those pills for years, well, ever since I met him. The same ones he had today—the yellow ones. I was always trying to get him to see a dermatologist, though actually most of the time I just told him to stop taking them at all. His skin was always fine. I couldn't understand why he bothered."

Joseph was slowly approaching the table, holding a jug of water and balancing two glasses in the other hand. Andrea leaned a little closer to Lata and said in a near-whisper, "One time, I tried throwing the pills away, and he went through the roof. I mean, he went totally ballistic. I figured he had an obsession about his skin, about the way he looks, you know?"

She gave a glance towards Joseph, patted Lata on the shoulder, and then jogged off in the direction she'd come from. Lata watched her round the rosemary bush and disappear from view. Skin problems? It was ludicrous. Joseph's skin was flawless and incredibly smooth. But then...had she ever heard Joseph out of breath? Even once?

"I'm so sorry about that," Joseph said, placing the jug on the table. "I thought she'd leave if I got up."

"She said your pills were for your skin." Lata snorted and raised an eyebrow, but Joseph looked away.

"She's obviously confused," he said. He poured them both a glass of water, missing his own glass slightly and spilling water on the glass tabletop.

"I know. Weird, eh? She said she was always trying to get you to see a dermatologist."

"She was always trying to get me to go to the gym more, too. She wasn't happy with the way I looked."

"That's awful. You never told me that." Lata reached across the table and held his hand.

"Yeah, well..." He shrugged, pulling his hand away.

"Strange though. She was with you for six years. Why would she think they were for your skin?"

"Look, I don't want to hear about what Andrea has to say," Joseph snapped, slamming his glass down. Lata jumped and looked around quickly at the nearby tables. "I don't like the woman, and I don't want her messing around with your mind. She's a manipulative bitch."

Lata sat in silence as Joseph drank a full glass of water, then poured himself another one, drumming his fingers on the table's surface. A mother and two children stood at the nearby pond, chucking bits of old bread to the ducks. Lata watched them until her homemade toasted muesli arrived.

After Sarah dropped her at the gate, Lata slipped inside and hung her umbrella on one of the hallway hooks, careful not to make a sound. Kicking off her wet shoes, she stood in the dark, kneading her forehead with her palms. The hallway clock ticked loudly.

What did it all mean? The pills weren't pharmaceutically recognized? They weren't for asthma? The smell of garlic and the sound of food frying wafted through the closed hallway door from the kitchen. She could hear Joseph humming as he cooked. She pulled the pill bottle from her pocket, the yellow pills rattling. A week ago, she'd have found it nearly inconceivable that Joseph would lie to her. Was he...what? Some sort of closet addict? But if he were an addict, surely he'd have hidden it from her entirely, not set his alarm eight times per day to take the pills right in front of her eyes. And anyway, Joseph didn't drink, let alone take weird drugs.

She heard footsteps approaching behind the hallway door and quickly darted into the bedroom, placing the pills on the bedside table beside the stack of other, identical bottles. Her heart raced.

"Is that you, babe?" Joseph called. A moment later, he flicked the light switch and stood in the bedroom doorway holding a glass of white wine. He was always so thoughtful. He had a way of holding wineglasses, his thumb and first finger tightly clasping the stems, his remaining fingers splayed like a fan. Usually she made fun of him.

"What a day!" he whistled. "I was worrying about you, out there. You know I counted seventeen, *seventeen* broken umbrellas this afternoon, stuffed into the bins along Queen Street."

Joseph carefully placed the wineglass upon his bedside table—next to his stockpile of pills—and held out his arms, waiting for her to step into his embrace. Lata leaned toward him and felt his arms curl around her. He smelled of garlic and washing powder.

"You okay?" he asked, kissing her hair.

"Yeah..." Lata screwed up her eyes. His arms were so warm and comforting. She hugged him back, squeezing tightly.

"What's wrong, babe? Did something happen at work?"

"Where do you get your pills?"

He held her out at arms' length and frowned down at her. "What's this obsession with my pills?"

"I just want to know."

"Well, I'd rather you stopped worrying about it. It's bad enough I have to take them every few hours without you reminding me of them, as well."

"I took them to be tested."

"You what?!" Joseph's face contorted. He let go of her and stormed from the room, slamming the door. Lata sunk onto the edge of their bed and held her face in her hands. Her socks were wet, and her feet felt cold on the wooden floor. Outside, a tin can flew rattling down the street.

A moment later, Joseph strode back in. "Lata, I can't believe this! Who did you give them to? Which one of your friends now thinks

I'm some sort of loony crackpot who's hooked on some weird drug? You *know* me. You know who I am. I can't believe you did this! I shouldn't have to explain every single aspect of my life to you. We're not chained together; we're not joined together like Siamese twins. We're separate people with separate lives. And I tell you everything, anyway! You know I see a Chinese guy for my back. You know that. Well, he's the one who gives them to me, isn't he? My god, what did you think? Western doctors never got it right. I went my whole life gasping and puffing until I tried these pills. I can't believe I even have to explain this to you. I'm, I'm utterly shocked and confused. Here I am, cooking for you, making *you* a dinner, pouring *you* a wine, pretty much going about my entire day with your happiness on my mind, yet you question me like I'm some sort of criminal! Maybe I shouldn't try so hard in the future."

He slammed the door again. A minute later, Lata heard the front door shut and the gate click.

Two weeks passed, and Lata didn't mention the pills. Joseph was right: she *knew* him. He wasn't the kind of guy to make up stories and lies. And since they'd had their argument, he'd made a point of telling her when he was going to see his Chinese guy, which had been twice already. Lata had never realized he saw him so regularly. Had she known that, then maybe it would have been obvious his pills weren't from a regular pharmacy. It explained the unlabeled bottles, too. She kicked herself for having ever listened to Andrea. You should never listen to your partner's ex—that's like Rule Number One of having a happy life.

It was a Friday evening, and Joseph was working late at the pool. Lata had just made herself a strongly sugared hot chocolate and switched on her laptop to check Facebook when her phone began to buzz. It was a call from an unknown number.

"Hello?"

"Lata, it's me, Sarah," Sarah whispered.

Lata felt a sudden surge of dread. She'd been avoiding Sarah's calls. The last thing she wanted was another conversation about those stupid pills. She should never have gone behind Joseph's back and shown them to her in the first place.

"Oh. Hi, Sarah. Um, look, sorry I haven't called you. I've been really—"

"I'm at work, so I've got to make this quick," Sarah cut in. "You've got to give me some of those pills. I've gotten into real trouble by giving them back to you. I said I'd lost them, but now the pharmacists are stressing out that someone might find them and mistake them for real medication and swallow one of them. They've had me search the entire premises three times already."

"Who would take a pill if they didn't know what it was?"

"Look, I know, it's paranoid, but I shouldn't have given them back to you. They want to run more tests, too. We've had someone from the Health Board come around. Everyone is freaking out that someone is manufacturing such poisonous pills."

"But they're not poisonous. Joseph takes them every day. And anyway, you don't need to worry. I found out they're Chinese herbal medicine."

"Chinese medicine? From where? Which doctor?"

"I...I don't know. Just some guy that Joseph goes to!"

"Look, can I just swing by now and get them from you? It'll save my butt, and to be honest, we do really need to know what they are. Joseph's health is at risk. In fact, you should get him to a hospital. Seriously, maybe it's better I tell everyone the truth."

"No! Please don't! I've already had an earful from Joseph about this. They're herbal; there's nothing wrong with them. Sarah, please just drop it. He's fine, honestly."

There was a pause. Lata could hear Sarah breathing.

"Okay," Sarah whispered at last. "But you should at least get him to go for a checkup. You know, to get some blood tests done. In case something is wrong."

"Okay, I promise I will," Lata said and hung up the phone.

Steam from her hot chocolate rose lazily in front of her eyes. She took a sip, but it tasted too sweet. Her laptop's screen saver had come on, and random photos were being propelled in random directions. Her old dog, Tasi. Roses from her grandmother's garden, back before she was put in a home. Her Uncle Mike's motorbike. A picture of her and Mary taken when they were kids. Lata clicked on this picture, halting its movement. Mary was holding an ice cream, and, judging by her face, Lata had already finished hers. They looked so cute in their orange headbands, their huge hair exploding like mushroom clouds around their faces. If something ever went wrong with Lata, Joseph could call Mary. He could call any member of her large family, and they'd either laugh at him and tell him he was worrying over nothing, or they'd all be piling into their cars and rushing over with thermometers and soup. But when something was wrong with Joseph, Lata had no one to call. He was an only child. He didn't speak to his parents. He didn't even have anything to show from his childhood, as it was all destroyed in a fire when he was eighteen.

Lata opened Google Images and ran a search for 'yellow pill.' She scrolled down past hundreds of photos, but none quite matched Joseph's pills, which were shaped like aspirin, yellow but not glossy, with nothing etched on their flat surfaces. She tried searching again, this time with 'yellow pill Chinese.' The results were even less likely.

Leaving her half-unfinished hot chocolate on the table, she went and fetched a bottle from Joseph's stash. Both the bottle and pills were frustratingly nondescript, with no unique identifying features. She tipped a pill onto her palm, sniffed it, then licked it with the tip of her tongue. Oh god! She threw it to the ground compulsively, saliva pooling in her mouth. It was the foulest thing she'd ever tasted. Her tongue felt like it was shrinking, curling up into the back of her mouth as if to shift itself further away from the horrible thing. Lata stooped to pick up the pill and held it gingerly between her thumb and finger. How could Joseph bear to eat these things eight times a day? His asthma must be really bad. For a second, she thought of Andrea and felt a rolling doubt in her stomach. But then she thought of Joseph, grabbed her hot chocolate, forced the pill into her mouth, and swallowed.

Joseph held her hand and shook it.

"I'm sure we've met before," he said. "At least, I think I've seen you around. Do you play squash?"

"Do I look like I play squash?" Lata asked, raising an eyebrow.

Joseph laughed. "I thought maybe I'd seen you at the gym where I work. I'm a swimming coach."

Lata looked him up and down. He was fit, wasn't he? "What was your name again?"

"Joseph."

They shimmied along the buffet table, holding their polished white plates. Lata was about to add several sausage rolls to what she now realized was a fried food fest on her plate, but, conscious of Joseph's elbow nudging her side, opted for salad instead. Joseph was busy piling seafood onto his own plate, apparently ignoring everything else.

"Are you a friend of Victor's?" He definitely wasn't a friend of Mary's. No handsome brown male friend of Mary's would have remained un-introduced for more than a second. Unless he was married.

"No, I'm a plus one," he said.

Lata sighed, nodded, and made to move away from the table.

"My friend's plus one," Joseph added, linking his arm in hers. "My friend Barry's, actually. He needs a sober driver, and I'm his only friend who doesn't drink."

Joseph led her outside to the balcony. A wide, white marble staircase extended to the lawns. A unicorn trotted between the sculpted hedges then disappeared.

"How come you can't have children?" Lata asked. She slipped her arms around his waist and held him tightly. "Unless you don't want to talk about it?"

"No, it's fine...I don't know really. It's some genetic thing. I'm just not fertile."

"Do you think you'd ever adopt?"

"Yeah...maybe. Look!" Joseph laughed and pointed to his plate. The calamari rings had eyes, which blinked slowly. Prawns scuttled around on their little tails. An enormous trout, which she hadn't noticed before, lay across Joseph's forearms. It raised its head to look at her, then opened its great flabby lips and screamed. Lata leapt backward.

"It's okay!" Joseph said, and with a wave of his arms he, and the trout, were gone.

Lata stood alone under a large blue sky. She felt something pinch her gut and looked down to see the sandy ground covered in thousands of pale, translucent crabs. Some of them were climbing up her white dress, clinging by their bulbous claws. Circles of blood appeared in the places where they pinched her. Shrieking, she tried to knock them off, but as she touched them, they stiffened like gargoyles, their pincers embedding themselves into her skin.

As she watched in horror, more and more crabs scuttled upwards, clambering over each other, and solidifying, until they formed a hideous crust across her abdomen. She felt the crab layer burning through her thin dress, rooting itself deeper inside her, tightening like a corset. She tugged at it, tried to get her fingers underneath, but the pain was unbearable.

"Get off! Get off!" she screamed, stumbling backwards, the crabs' shells crunching beneath her feet.

She turned and immediately fell over a deck chair sitting in the sand.

"This is the life, isn't it?" Joseph said. He held a green coconut in his hand with a straw poking from the top, but his features were shadowed beneath a wide-brimmed straw hat. "If I'd known it was this good over here, I would have come sooner."

Lata collapsed onto one of the other deck chairs, all lined up and facing the surf. Water sparkled brightly beyond the shade of the palm trees. Pain spread upward through her body, into her chest, into her arms. Her throat felt so dry that she gagged.

"Didn't you ever come here as a kid?" She heard herself say and noticed that there she was, dressed in her swimsuit, perched at the end of the chair, facing Joseph.

"Nah." Joseph sucked on his straw.

"Where did you go, you know, on family holidays?"

"Nowhere."

"Nowhere?"

"Nowhere special. It's not worth talking about."

"I'd like to. Talk about it, I mean."

"We should go for a swim." Joseph grabbed her hand—her other hand, on her other self—and pulled her to her feet. A pelican lifted itself heavily into the air, winking at both of her as it passed.

"Help me," Lata whispered.

Her other self shook her head and rolled her eyes. "Oh my god, Joseph, you've barely gotten out of the water! I thought we were going to work on our tans."

Holding hands, the two of them walked out into the glittering ocean, their forms becoming smaller and smaller until they disappeared altogether.

Lata rolled off the deck chairc and crawled towards the coconut Joseph had left lying on the sand. The inside of her mouth felt like dried, cracked mud. She lifted the coconut to her mouth, tilting back her neck, and felt a cascade of sand slide across her dry tongue. Retching, unable to breathe, she reached inside her mouth with her fingers, frantically scooping sand back out. She felt something tug, like wet paper tearing, and pulled out a long, shriveled chunk of meat into her hands.

"Lata! Speak to me. Speak to me, Lata! Oh god, what have you done?"

Joseph was prodding her, shaking her shoulder. Lata couldn't move. The universe had shrunk down to one small, tightly compressed ball of darkness and pain, and she was curled inside it, eyes shut. Her mouth was a pit of pure, white fire, as if chili oil had been smeared across cauterized gums. Her skin felt as thin and dry as rice paper, stretched tightly across her bones. She slowly became aware of the fact that her arms were wrapped around her belly, and that she held secure a sticky mess beneath. She hugged her tummy tighter. Everything smelled and tasted of blood.

Something hard slid beneath her back.

"It's okay, babe; it's okay," Joseph said into her ear. His breath was loud and fast.

He slipped another arm beneath her legs.

"No—" Lata gurgled, a mouthful of thick foam bubbling from between her teeth. A stream of something else then rushed from her mouth, beyond her control. It felt cool on her chin and neck.

She felt herself being lifted and placed back down. The sound of a tap running. A line of cold water rising against her legs. A glass thrust to her mouth, and a palm on her forehead, bending her head backward.

Sometimes she woke long enough to observe her body grow heavier as the cocoon of water surrounding her drained away and then become light again as it swirled around her, creeping up her torso like a thousand spiders, rushing into her pores. Other times, she woke to the sound of her teeth chattering.

When Lata finally opened her eyes, it took a moment to realize why the scene looked wrong. She lay fully dressed in their bath, submerged up to her neck in steaming water. But it was the water itself. It was too dark.

She tenderly touched her abdomen, wincing, then raised her wrinkled hands to her face. A thick flaky crust coated the inside of her nostrils, down her chin, right down her neck. The front of her shirt was stained a dark brown.

"Joseph?" she called, the sound coming out as a raspy whisper.

He came to the door quickly, brow creased, his brown eyes wide. Another man followed him to the door, looked in, met Lata's eyes, and retreated.

As Joseph knelt down beside the bath, Lata began to cry.

"Shhh," he said, bending to kiss her forehead. "You'll be okay."

"I need—" Lata began but coughed a small clot of blood into her mouth and spat it into the bath. "Hospital."

"My doctor has seen you. We've given you some medicine."

Joseph hung his head. When he raised his face again, his eyes were wet. "I'm sorry, Lata. This is all my fault. I shouldn't have left the pills lying about. I should have warned you about how dangerous they were. I'm so sorry."

"Please, Joseph. Take me to a hospital."

"My doctor is very good," Joseph said, smoothing down her hair. "They won't know how to deal with this in a hospital. You're better off here with me."

"Joseph, for fuck's sake!" Lata choked. "Get me to a hospital!"

Lata emptied the last pill onto her hand. It was long, thin, and brown from an unlabeled bottle. She'd taken them for four months, three per day as prescribed by the so-called "Chinese doctor" she couldn't remember ever actually meeting. Joseph wouldn't reveal where he went to buy the pills, but they'd never run out, and he'd never let her forget to take them.

"Hey, babe, it's getting dark. We should go."

Joseph stood at the front door in his shorts and running shoes. He was already flexing his legs, his finger poised above his stopwatch, set to time their progress. Smiling, Lata tutted and rolled her eyes. This was part of her routine now, too—exercising to strengthen her damaged lungs. Joseph's enthusiasm and dedication was sweet, if not a little irritating. She took one last look at the bottle in her hand then threw it into the recycling bin.

The streetlights were on, and a lone star squatted confidently in the clear blue sky. Venus, Lata thought. She had no idea where she'd learned that—she'd never taken an interest in astronomy—but she knew that the first bright star seen in the early evening was Venus. Venus was also the Roman goddess of love. But if that was the case, why was she sitting there all alone?

As they turned the corner and passed the dark windows of the vacant dairy, Lara slowed down a little to properly glimpse her reflection. Damn, girl! If she turned side on to the sun, she wouldn't cast a shadow at all. She patted her midriff, glad that the skin had finally healed. Hopefully the scarring would fade a bit, especially now that she finally had a figure she'd want to show off.

She'd been forced to take nearly four weeks off work; she'd nearly lost her job. Her family had been beside themselves with worry. Her mother and Mary had taken it in turns to sit beside her bed until she was well enough to hold a spoon and walk to the toilet by herself. Joseph had explained to them—to all of them, to anyone who'd asked—that his pills didn't suit everyone's constitutions. Her mother had been livid. "Lata, what were you thinking, taking medicine not prescribed for you?" Every time she called now, she spent a good five minutes praising Joseph for being such a good man, for looking after her foolish daughter so well.

Joseph ran up and down the darkening streets, his legs pumping up and down like some mechanical creature in an Eveready ad. Lata followed, her breath becoming haggard, a line of sweat forming on her upper lip. She really wasn't feeling up to this. And it felt like she was attacking her lungs, not helping them! She'd had a terrible night's sleep, waking from another nightmare. Damn it. Lata shook her head, trying to clear from her mind the images that came suddenly surging up. A void of utter darkness. A light flashing across it. A bronze statue of Joseph, his face torn off. The hollows where his eyes and nose should be, green with age...

Lata leaped over the low fence surrounding the rugby field and gasped her way across the field and past the children's playground. To her right were the parallel bars where the insane runners did pull ups; thankfully, there were none there to see her today. The oak trees lining the park were bushy with new leaves, daffodils clustering around their roots. Maybe she could pick some tomorrow. Was that allowed? She and Mary used to love visiting Uncle Mike's place because of the daffodils. He'd owned a blue plastic tea party set, god knows why, and they used to sit out amongst the golden flowers, sipping Raro like English royalty.

"Wait," Lata called, coming to a sudden stop at the edge of the floodlit skate park, doubled up and leaning against her thighs. A trio of teenage girls sat on the edge of the bowl, a box of watermelon-colored RTDs only half hidden beneath a black hoodie, a thin thread of cigarette smoke passing between them.

Joseph retraced his steps.

"Have you had enough?"

Lata nodded, unable to speak.

"Let's just run home," he said, rubbing her back. "It's not far."

As Lata pulled herself upright, brushing his hand away, Joseph's alarm went off. He stood on his toes for a moment, peering around the illuminated concrete structure, until he spotted the water fountain at the far edge of the skate park. He took off at a quick jog, Lata following at a walk. As he pushed the pill into his mouth, Lata watched, fascinated and horrified. He didn't even flinch. He never did. In fact, after swallowing a mouthful of water and wiping his face, he actually grinned. Lata looked away, screwing up her face. She heard him jog up behind her but took off at a run so he didn't try and hug her.

It was dark by the time they got home. Joseph pulled off his clothes and threw them into the washing basket in the bathroom, first placing his bottle of pills on the coffee table in the lounge. Lata heard the shower turn on, followed by the sound of Joseph humming.

She stared at the pill bottle. It wasn't right. She didn't know what it was, but something wasn't right.

Snatching up the bottle in her hand, she headed to the kitchen. She found the aspirin quickly, inside the first aid lunch box along with the Vicks VapoRub, and about fifty Band-Aids too small to realistically use. Standing on tiptoes, she rifled through the cupboard, listening carefully to the running water of the shower, pushing aside the box of ice cream cones and the apple cider vinegar, hurriedly searching the back of the top shelf, packed tight with the things they'd bought and then forgotten about. Aha, there! She grabbed the yellow food coloring, held it up to the light to judge its hue, then slipped it into her pocket.

When Joseph's alarm went off in the middle of the night, Lata nearly slept through it. But then she remembered. She held her breath, heart beating fast, as she listened to Joseph unscrewing the pill bottle and a moment later, the sound of his glass thumping back down onto the bedside table. Eyes wide open in the dark, stomach churning, she lay rigid and silent.

Nothing happened. She focused her attention on the hall clock, counting the seconds as minute after minute passed. Down the hall and through the kitchen, a tap dripped. Joseph snuffled quietly. A car drove past outside, the headlights illuminating a quick arc of their ceiling.

Lata turned over, exhaling loudly as she closed her eyes. What did she expect? The pills were just for his asthma. He wasn't going to have an asthma attack while sleeping peacefully in his bed. What a stupidly idiotic thing for her to do. This was up there—top of her list of dumb ideas never to admit to anyone.

As Lata feel asleep, she felt a wide smile stretch across her face and felt all the muscles in her body relax for what felt like the first time in months.

Lata was woken by glass being smashed.

The bedsheets were thrashing, like someone was standing at the end of the bed, shaking them. It sounded like everything in the room was crashing to the ground.

"Joseph, what's happening? I think we're having an earthquake!"

Lata reached out to touch him but felt something large and slimy slap against her arm.

She leapt out of bed and switched on the light.

In the bed, where Joseph should have been, lay an enormous squid. Its eye looked like a black-centered poached egg, lopsided and bulging. Its broad tentacles were brown, the undersides pale and striped with fleshly suckers that resembled beige fungi. Some of the tentacles were still trapped beneath the writhing blankets, while the others butted at the items on Joseph's beside table, knocking pill bottles and photo frames to the floor.

"Oh my god!" Lata screamed, hands to her face. "Oh my god!"

The thing seemed to look at her then, and raising itself up on one folded tentacle, the rest of the tentacles opened like an anemone. At the core gaped a hideous hole with a circle of black teeth. The mouth stretched wider—fleshy gaps appearing between the pointed teeth— wide enough to engulf her leg.

Lata screamed.

The creature collapsed onto its side again, tentacles still jerking at Joseph's bedside table. As the last pill bottle rolled to the floor, the thing curled its tentacles around the bed's side, and hauled itself on to the floor. As it dragged itself along the polished floorboards, a dark trail of blood slid out behind, several large shards of Joseph's broken glass visibly embedded into its underside.

Joseph.

It reared its enormous head up, opening its tentacles wide once more and opening its mouth, then collapsed on to an unopened bottle of pills. Lata heard the distinct crack of plastic.

And then, as if suddenly having lost its energy, the creature flopped on to its side. The pill bottle rolled out from between its twitching tentacles like an egg.

"No!" Lata screamed. "Joseph! No, no, no!"

She dropped to her knees and crawled to its side, her hands fumbling as she tried to hurriedly open the pill bottle's lid.

"Oh come on!" she cried, spilling half the pills onto the ground.

Finally tipping one into her hand, she thrust it against Joseph's huge, sleek head. "Take it! Take it!"

But as she tugged aside his heavy tentacles, trying to locate his mouth, she realized it was too late. He had fallen still, and his eyes were blank disks.

)O(O( )O(O( )O(O( )O(

ABOUT THE AUTHOR

I.K. Paterson-Harkness lives on a grimy street in the center of Auckland, New Zealand, watching seagulls squabble on the Chinese supermarket roof across the road while she tries to write her stories. With university degrees in music, philosophy, and creative writing, she doesn't quite know what to do with herself. Mostly, when not writing, she's doodling on a pad or thinking about time travel.

Spouse Swap

Cooper O'Connor

1.

Mondays at eight, you can watch alleged celebrities binge themselves silly on *Celebrity Food Fights!* On Wednesdays, you can watch other celebrities *shrink* themselves silly on a series of supposedly life-threatening activities on *Celebrity Die-it!* And on Fridays, you can watch wives trade husbands on *Spouse Swap*.

If I look familiar, that's probably where you know me from.

You're probably asking yourself why I signed up for it. The answer is both easy and unglamorous. Sylvia wanted to, and I'm a terribly weak man. There's an invisible sign that hangs above our front door, and I'm the only one who can see it: What Sylvia wants, Sylvia gets.

Sylvia loves reality TV shows. She loves the dancing ones, the singing ones, the gross-out ones, the ones with people in a house manufacturing drama. She even likes one called *Adulterers* with your host Bobby Lodge. Even by reality TV standards, that show is pretty low.

Sylvia was a lot more fun when we first started seeing each other. I'm not a very picky man and didn't mind that Sylvia wasn't the best looker. That never mattered to me, which is why I thought it was ridiculous when she started thinking about plastic surgery. About two years ago, Sylvia had nose reduction surgery. In her mind, it never happened and denies it every time I bring it up, even though I'm the one who paid for it.

It's funny how we go through our lives trying to convince ourselves that the lies we tell ourselves are really the truth. Take, for instance, the daily lies Sylvia and I share with each other:

"I love you," I lie.

"I love you, too," she lies back.

But we still tell ourselves it's the truth.

Sylvia's changed since I met her. To be fair, she wasn't ready to be a mother. When you're young and idealistic, you think you can lift the world up with nothing but the strength of your own love. That's fine and good, but when you're jerked from what you used to call sleep at two in the morning to wipe shit out of your baby's ass and your friends don't call you anymore because there's no point in asking if you want to come out, because you have a kid and don't have a sitter, well…you begin to feel less like Atlas and more like Popeye without a can of spinach anywhere in sight.

And in her defense, life hadn't turned out the way she'd planned. She was shorter than she wanted to be, fatter than she wanted to be, with one more kid than she wanted to have, married to a house painter.

To make up for those things that she has no control over, she usurped all the power of the marriage and rules the house with a tyranny that would make Kim Jong-il jealous. Take, for instance, the spare room next to the bathroom that used to be my studio. About six years ago, Sylvia needed a room for her wardrobe, so I was demoted to the basement among the tools, boxes, spiders and dusty Gazelle that she bought to shed off the baby weight and used only once. I like to paint, you see. Once upon a time, I wanted to be an artist. I never talk to Sylvia about art. She never understood it. She used to like it when I drew funny pictures of the two of us but never really cared *why* I did it. I've given up trying to explain to her the meditative joy that comes from the wet scrape of a brush stroke along the canvas. All I've ever gotten has been a bored stare in return. I've given up trying. So if creativity calls, you can find me hunched in the corner of the basement with the tools, boxes, spiders, and Gazelle to keep me company. At least they understand.

Most of my paintings sit in a dusty pile in the basement. I've long since quit bothering to ask her if I can hang them in our house. She's never said *no*, mind you, but the way her face would squish disapproval was enough of an answer. I didn't want her to hang a painting only for her to redirect her irritation at me down the road over some other subject, like the time I slept on the couch for two weeks after I forgot to pick up the paper towels at the store like she'd asked. Of course, it wasn't about the paper towels. It's never about the paper towels, is it? So I've learned by now that when I see her face squish like that, I just give her what she wants. Invisible sign, remember?

She's only allowed one painting to go up. It's of a young girl on a bicycle, riding down a path cut through a field of dandelions. I can see why Sylvia likes it. I imagine that a part of her looks at the girl and wishes she was that child with a future as open and bright as that field of dandelions.

I don't paint much anymore. Between the houses and Dylan, I just don't have the time. The possibility of my work ever starring in a show hasn't just grown cold, its frozen somewhere out in fucking Northern Siberia, and I'd be lying if I didn't reach for the carrot she dangled in front of me when she said, "Just think about it, Dan. If we do this, then you can show everyone how *good* you are. Everyone will want to see *more*. This could be your *chance*. Don't you want to take it?"

It'd be more valiant if I said that's why I agreed to do it. But the truth is, it's easier to just agree with Sylvia. Even if that means signing yourself over for a reality TV show. At least this meant I wouldn't have to see her for two weeks.

You've probably seen the show. There are a few of them. That's the thing that gets me the most. Why settle for one show about swapping wives and husbands when you can have *three*? Hell, even HBO has a show called *Swingers*. You can imagine where the differences between that show and the others ones are. Anyway, the premise is this: you take two families and switch the wives for a week. Film the shenanigans that result from the differences each wife brings to the family. It's simple enough, and besides, like Sylvia says, it's going to make me a *star*.

By the way, I know that Sylvia doesn't care about whether my paintings sell. She'd care if I were successful enough to take her out to fancier restaurants and pay for lipo, boob jobs, cheek implants, hair extensions and lip injections. Sylvia only cares at becoming famous and hopefully breaking out of the shitty existence life boxed her into. And I'm okay with that.

Don't get me wrong. I don't hate my life. I just don't happen to like it very much, either. I only have one real escape. Once a week, I go to a shooting range. My dad always liked guns. He's dead now. Cancer, about ten years now. It might be loud down at the range, but it's really my only quiet time. And when I'm there, I feel like he's there with me. Sylvia always yelled at me about how loose I was with keeping the gun. It sat in a box on the top shelf of the closet with a spare clip sitting next to it. Dylan was too short to reach it, not that he'd ever leave his PSP long enough to every try. Beside, I think I kept it there as an invitation for Sylvia to put me out of my misery.

2.

The producer's name is Slelsnack. I don't know what kind of name that is. Polish maybe. Possibly Martian. I shouldn't be too hard on Arnie. After all, with a name like his, what else could he do with his life other than produce reality television shows? I mean, he wasn't fortunate enough to be born with the name Carlyle or Rutherford. No one will be naming a museum after old Arnie. And if by chance, I ever see a Slelsnack Historical Center for Reality Television Programming, I'll be sure to hurry on my damned way. Maybe I'll whistle the theme to *Cheers* to ward off the evil spirits that will no doubt lurk within its exploitative and fluorescent-lit walls. It doesn't have to be *Cheers*, of course. It could be the theme to *Growing Pains, Family Ties,* or *The Andy Griffith Show*. Whatever song you choose to invoke is up to you. Just so long as it's from a time when television wasn't about grown men and women whoring themselves out for the world to see for a chance to become *famous.*

Slelsnack pushes his way past the cameraman as he makes his way toward me. I find it strange and invasive the way his feet trample the carpet, the way the cameramen block the doorways. I hope this experience doesn't affect Dylan's development, somehow.

Slelsnack checks his watch. "Dan, Dan, the painter man. We're going to roll soon. You know what to do, right? The three of you are going to have a weepy good-bye, and then Sylvia's gonna' come with us. Make sure you make it good for the cameras, okay? The audience loves a sad good-bye. It makes it that much sweeter when you two get back together, you know what I'm saying?"

"Yeah," I said. "I know what you're saying."

Slelsnack grins and whops me on the shoulder. I can't help but check to see if he's left a handprint. I tell myself to burn the shirt and scrub the skin beneath it when I get the chance.

"This episode's gonna' change your life. I've seen it happen. It won't be the same after this. You're going places!"

"Sure," I say. "Can't wait."

"Your mike feel okay?"

"Yeah, the mike feels fine."

"Oh, Arnie, leave him alone," says Sylvia. "Dan doesn't *like* the spotlight."

Neither should you, I want to tell her. *It shows all your wrinkles and the little moustache you forgot to wax at the corner of your lip.*

She bends down and kisses me on the cheek. "I'm going to miss you," she says and god damn, she even has tears in her eyes.

"The camera's not rolling yet," I say. "Don't waste them."

"Oh, Dan," she says and strokes my face. "I know how you didn't want to do this. You know I appreciate you doing this, right?"

"Sure, Syl. No biggie."

"You're so sweet!" she says and kisses me again. Twice in a day? I wonder if she's going for a record.

"When I get back, we'll celebrate, okay?" She straightens up and turns to Arnie. "Okay, Arnie. I'm ready."

Within the minute, we're on the lawn while the camera guys, Hank and Larry, roll footage. We pretend to be a happy couple in front of our guests. She gives me a long, slow, tearful kiss as she stands beside the waiting limousine. Dylan stands next to me, bored, with face out of his PSP long enough to stick a finger up his nose. Sylvia doesn't notice. When she sees the footage, she's going to flip that her great performance was ruined by nothing more than an index finger and a nostril. Inside, I'm beaming. That's my boy.

"Oh, Dan," she breathes. "I love you so much. I love you so, so much."

"I love you, too, honey," I say.

"I can't stand to be away from you!"

"Me neither, honey."

"Oh, Dan. Dan. I'll miss you."

"I'll miss you, too."

"Don't go falling in love," she says.

With that, unable to bear the good-bye any longer, she flings herself into the limousine and turns her head away from us while the tears pour from her stoic face. She's putting on a good show. I want to see her do it with a southern accent, Blanche Dubois style. I want to see her *swoon*.

They film Dylan and me as we watch the limousine pull away and drive out of sight. I catch a glance at Slelsnack who's staring at my son with a scowl on his face. He's mad Dylan isn't crying. As he has informed us at every opportunity: "Tears equal ratings."

If Dylan is upset his mother just drove away for two weeks, he doesn't show it. In fact, he gives a big yawn and looks at me with bored, tired eyes. "I'm hungry," he tells me.

About twenty minutes and a few bologna sandwiches later, Slelsnack approaches me.

"Dan, Dan the family man," he says. "We're about to bring in your new wife. We need you and Dylan in the living room. Follow me." With that, he walks us to the couch and gives us the following directions:

"You two sit on the couch. Good. Now pretend you're talking. But don't talk and don't move your lips. Dan, lean into the couch like you just got home from work. Dylan move closer to your dad. Not *too* close. Like, not *weird* close, got me? We don't want to give the wrong impression. It's a family show after all. Good, now you're just spending some time together. Don't look at each other. Make it look natural. Pretend I'm not even here. Dan, move a little to the left. Just a little. Move your right arm. No, up…like …there you go. Dylan, sit up. No, not that much. You look like a little nerd when you do that. We want to go for a cool kid angle. Actually, can you lose the glasses? Oh, he can't see? Do you think that'd be a problem?"

Once he's moved us into a pose he's satisfied with, he continues his directions. "Now remember not to talk because we can't have any interruptions. The focus is going to be on *her*. When she comes in, do what's natural. You know, introduce yourself. If you want to lay down the law, that'd be good. It'll make *conflict*, and conflict sells. Conflict equals ratings. Remember that."

"I thought tears equals ratings."

A crooked Hollywood smile erupts on his face. "Yeah, sure," he said. "Lots of things equal ratings. Tears, conflict, sex. You want to go for all three, Dan, I'm not going to stop you."

"What'd you do before you were a reality producer, Arnie? You didn't by chance, I don't know, hang out in trees and offer forbidden apples to anyone did you?"

"With a wit like that, we could get you your own show in no time."

After a minute of talking to the cameramen, Arnie runs in front of us and tells us that my new wife is about to enter the house.

And then, right on cue, enters Suzanne.

She's clutching a bag with both hands in front of her. A yellow streak runs through her black hair like a lightning bolt in the night sky. Tattoos cover one arm and the tops of her sandaled feet. I can tell she's wearing little to no make up. A loose lock of raven dark hair falls in front of her face. I resist the urge to run up to her and curl it behind her ear.

She looks at me, tilting her head to the side. A soft smile stretches across her face.

"Hi?" she says, and she laughs. "I don't know what to do! Oh my god, I'm so nervous. I'm Suzanne."

I push off from the couch and cross the living room to where she stands. For a moment, I forget about Slelsnack and the cameramen. I reach out my hand. She takes it. Her hand is soft, her grip light but firm.

"Suzanne," I repeat. "I'm Dan." I turn back to the couch. Later, when I watch the footage I laugh at the dopey grin that stretches ear to ear.

"Dylan," I say. "Meet your new mom."

3.

Later that night, Dylan has gone to bed while Suzanne and I sit at the kitchen table. It's the first time we haven't been given directions on what to say, what to do. Once cameras stopped rolling on her entrance, Slelsnack gave her directions on what to say and do as she explored the house and went through Sylvia's stuff. Was it strange I didn't care that a stranger poked and prodded through Sylvia's most personal items?

Now, the dinner table. I'm sitting across from a complete stranger, and I'm supposed to make this look natural. Larry and Hank continue to roll footage. I don't know where Slelsnack is, and I really don't care.

Before long, I ask her why she wanted to be on the show.

She's quiet for a moment before she answers. She stretches her arms across the table and folds her fingers together in a way that makes me think of an alley cat strutting across a ramshackle fence on a secret midnight escapade. The image is so vivid, I realize I'm sketching it on the back of the envelope for the gas bill.

"My husband Mark, he's…no, let me start over. I don't know how things are between you and Sylvia, but things aren't great for Mark and me. What I mean by that…I don't want to say anything bad about him. I really don't because that wouldn't be fair…but things have *changed* for us since we got married. I don't know if that makes sense. Mark opened up a tattoo parlor about a year ago, and since then, he's been nothing but business. Making calls, setting up appointments. He works all the time, even when he's home. We never go out anymore. We never have any *fun*. I know he's trying to make a solid business. Even though he has a lot of clients, he's losing too much money. So I thought maybe if I signed up for the show, I could help him get some business and maybe understand him a little bit better? And distance makes the heart grow fonder, they say." She stops only because she must see the cloud that had passed over my face. She cocks her head. A lock of hair falls. "What's with that face?"

She bites her lip. "Oh god, did I say something offensive already?"

I shake my head. "No, what you just said. It wasn't offensive. You just laid it all out on the table. I'm not used to that kind of truth around here."

Her eyes flick to the camera, and she begins to blush. "Did I say too much? I said too much didn't I?"

"I'm the wrong guy to ask. Besides…" I trail off, and another image pops into my head.

"Hey, why are you laughing?"

"I'm sorry." I wipe an eye. "It's the thought of Sylvia living with a tattoo artist. It's just so un-Sylvia."

She smiles at me. It's soft, shy, half-hidden behind a falling cascade of hair. "That's the point of the show, Dan. You know. A couple people from different lives switch places? Point a camera and record the shocked looks on their faces."

"You're right. I guess it just doesn't seem…well, I mean I hope you don't find it shocking to be here."

"Shocking? No, not *shocking*." She looks around, nibbles her lip. "It's just a little…"

"Boring?"

"*Thank* you. I didn't want to say it. I'm sorry. I shouldn't have said that. That's rude. Does that make me bad?"

"It makes you honest. More honest than I've been, I have to say."

"It's not all boring, I guess. I do like that," she says and points to a painting on the wall.

"That's mine," I tell her.

She looks back at it, then back to me. "Wait, you mean you *painted* it?"

"I'm a painter. Houses, mostly. Well, always, actually. But I dabble on canvas when I can."

She must see something in my face, a pain that I've long since learned to swallow because she reaches out and puts her hand over mine. With a squeeze she forces me to look into her winter blue eyes.

"Something I've learned in life? We're not defined by what we're paid to do but what we *love* to do. It doesn't *matter* if you get paid for the things you love to do," she tells me. "When it comes to artists, it's *who you are*. Painters are painters regardless of how much money they make." She squeezes my hand one more time and lets go. "Do you have any more?"

"Sure. Yeah." I stumble over my words. This is foreign to me. Alien, like Sleslnack. Sudden embarrassment slow burns through my body and tingles the surface of my skin. "Not hanging up, though."

"Why not? Embarrassed?"

"Yeah, actually," I say. Though it's the truth in the moment, it isn't the reason the paintings aren't hanging throughout the house, but I drop it.

"Can I see them?"

"Do you really want to?"

"Of course I do!"

"Wait here," I find myself saying against better judgment. It's as if Sleslnack remote controls my body, and although I want to go run and hide under the bed away from this inked-up stranger and the cameras, I watch myself descend into the basement to pull out pieces of myself that have been submerged in darkness for so long, I'm half afraid they will burn up the second I step into the kitchen light.

In a few minutes I'm back with a large leather portfolio case in one hand and a stack of canvases in the other. I stand in front of her and the cameras and I don't know what do to.

She has to notice my hesitation. She gives a gentle smile and pats the chair next to her.

I look over her shoulder as she goes through each one. She takes her time, and she's silent. Every now and then, she reaches out to touch one and stops herself before she does. I want to tell her she can. I want her to, but I don't want to break the silence of the moment.

Suddenly she stops at one of the canvases. The painting depicts a man on a snowy evening, resting beside a road and gazing into the warm glowing window of a house where a family sits around a table.

"I really like this," she says. She holds it as though it's a cloudy dream she wants to take with her into the waking world, afraid the morning breezes will blow it away.

"You can have it," I tell her before I know what I'm saying.

She looks at me over her shoulder and puts it on the table. "I couldn't," she says.

I pick it up and hand it to her. "It's not mine anymore," I say. "Consider it my gift to you. You can hang it up in Mark's tattoo parlor."

"No. I won't. I'm going to hang it in the house. Above the TV where everyone can see it."

She takes it from me. I'm very aware of how our fingers brush lightly in the exchange.

"This is beautiful," she says. She stands up and faces me. She opens her arms and hugs me. "Thank you, Dan," she says as she presses her head into my shoulder. "I wish I had something to give you in return."

She breaks the embrace. "I'm going to bed now," she says. "It's been a long day."

"Yes," I say. "It certainly has."

"Well, good night, Dan."

"Good night, Suzanne."

Just before she vanishes from sight, she flashes me a smile and a wave.

And then she's gone to sleep in my wife's bed while I take the couch.

While I fall asleep, I think about the appreciation in her eyes as I gave her the picture. She understands. Like the spider, the tools, the dusty boxes, and the Gazelle. She understands.

Not like Sylvia.

Not like Sylvia at all.

4.

She stands facing me, her back to a stove on whose burners waft heat waves the colors of peas and butter and corn on the cob. It's that perfect time of September when it's still hot enough to enjoy the foods of summer, but just enough chill in the air to begin to sample the dinners the late fall and early winter will bring.

"I want to make a deal with you," she says. "Think about it real hard, because I'm going to be honest. I want you to say 'yes' to this."

She pushes a curl of raven-colored hair behind her ear and tips her head to her side. "The deal is, every night I'm here, I'll cook. *Huge* dinners. *And* desert!" Her eyes pop like rockets on the Fourth of July, and a smile flares across her face. "I'll have to make my cake before I leave. Oh my god, you'll love it." Her eyes close; she smiles. "So soft. So moist. I can't *wait*." Her eyes open. Lock on mine. "There's only one stipulation," she says, and she points. "*You* clean. I *hate* doing dishes."

I reach into the fridge and pull out two beers. I crack open the first beer, grinning at the free advertisement I'm giving to Sam Adams. I pop the top to the second beer and hand it to her, saying, "Look, you can cut the act now. Dinners, deserts. Every night? There's no way you do all this back at home."

As she takes the cold beer from my hands, I watch as her smile falters and the stars in her eyes fizzle as they fall back down to earth.

"I don't," she sighs, and I feel a flash of guilt for dousing the light in those eyes. "You're right. We do take out a lot. Our schedules are so different; Mark and I don't even really eat together as much as we'd like."

She looks back at me, and the lights in her eyes ignite once more. "But I thought that since I'm here, I might as well pick up some good habits!" Her slender hand hides in the mitten embrace of the oven glove. She holds a spoon and wiggles it at me. "Come on. You *know* you want *to*."

I reach back into the fridge and grab a soda. Talking to her over my shoulder, I walk to the kitchen table where Dylan sits, playing his ever-present PSP. I *thunk* the soda can down in front of him. If he notices me, he doesn't show it.

"I just don't want you to do anything you don't want to do," I tell her. "You don't have to cook dinner if you don't want to is what I'm saying."

I resume my spot against the counter in front of the microwave. I can't tell you the last time I stood in the kitchen with Sylvia while she cooked. On those rare occasions when she did cook, you would find me on the couch, watching TV or in the basement, living out the sad excuse of what used to be a dream. But being here, immersed in the aromas and the banter, I find revelation in the simple joy of being *in the moment*. I relish it as much as I can feel my taste buds quiver with anticipation for the forthcoming food.

"But I *do* want to cook dinner." She makes a fist and props it upon her hip. "Be honest; you're not one of those intellectuals who think that women shouldn't cook because it perpetuates some stereotype, are you? Just cause I'm a modern woman doesn't mean that I don't want to get right down to dinner, you know what I'm saying, Dan?"

"I'm not disagreeing. I just want to make sure. If you're more comfortable with take-out or eating out, then that's what we'll do."

She comes to me and pins me against the counter. She stabs her finger into my chest with an authoritative poke. "I *want* to," she purrs. "I cook. You clean."

"If you want to role play this particular domestic fantasy, I'm one hundred percent down with that. I'll accept your offer, but *I* have a stipulation."

She raises an eyebrow while a smile teases the corners of her mouth. "Oh? What's on your mind?"

"I'll clean up. You cook dinners. Just like you want." I put my finger in the air and hold it in front of her face. "But I'll cook breakfast." She rolls her eyes and walks to the burners to stir the carrots.

"I'm not finished," I said. "Like I said, I get breakfasts. If you want to be fair about it, you can clean. For dinner, I don't care if you're roasting a pig in the yard. I won't lift a finger to help you."

Turning back to me, her face is a winking moon sliding behind the hill of her shoulder. "Okay then," she says with a satisfied smile. "Now, I want to try new recipes that I can take home with me. So you need to tell me if anything sucks."

"I don't have a problem with that."

She whirls around and once again threatens me with the spoon. "*Promise* me. Don't do that thing that most guys do, you know, that thing where you think you should never say, 'Yes,' if a woman asks if *this* makes her fat. I don't want to go back with crappy recipes. So if something's overcooked, or if you think I put too much garlic or whatever, you tell me."

"I'm telling you, I'll tell you if your food sucks. Besides, my mother said I was half-vampire I hate garlic so much. So if you put too much garlic in something, I'll make sure you know."

She shoots me a glance before turning back to stir the veggies. "I'll keep that in mind. Vampire. Got it. Producers never told me about *that* before I came onto the show. I would have made sure to pack my stake and a cross. I'm not going to have to worry about you sneaking into my room in the middle of the night to suck on my neck am I?"

I open the cabinet closest to me and reach in. I throw her the garlic. "Here you go," I say. "Now you're safe from my insidious clutches."

"Thanks. I still want to talk to the producers about their lapse in judgment."

"You're really surprised Slelsnack didn't tell you to come prepared? You don't think a stake and cross make *him* nervous?"

Her eyes widen and she turns to me with her mouth in an O, as if to say, "Aw naw you dinnit!" And then she sees Slelsnack behind me, out of the camera's view. He stands unsure of whether or not he should laugh or be offended. And while he works out it, I watch her watch him rock back and forth on each foot like he has to pee. Then she snickers. Then she begins to laugh.

And I turn, and I now see him, except now he is frozen. I wonder if he thinks the cameras would swoop in on him and flash his embarrassment on TV's nationwide the way he'd done to so many people before.

And then I began to laugh.

And Dylan watches from the dinner table. If I were him, I'd have already begun to question the definition of reality. I know I did. Not until much later.

But by then it was too late.

5.

My life begins to orbit around our meals like the earth around the sun. I'd never been an "eat at the kitchen table" kind of guy, but like many other things, Suzanne was opening up worlds of undiscovered joys that had previously gone unnoticed. Cooking and cleaning became less of a chore and evolved into part of a process. She and I were two parts of a machine. Our actions kept it running. You see, we found that we genuinely got along. There was none of the painful self-awareness that comes from trying to impress someone. I was married. She was married. It was safe.

Although we both knew our pairing was ultimately staged for the entertainment of middle America, every meal was one less meal we would have together before she left my house, and I found myself affected by this thought.

"Dan," she says suddenly over breakfast. "I'm going to shoot straight with you. I don't think I'd like your wife very much."

I rotate my coffee mug on the kitchen table, unsure how to respond. I've grown more accustomed to Suzanne to the point where she feels like close friend rather than a stranger, but I'm still aware of the two men crouched in the periphery of my vision with large, boxy, black tumors that sit upon their shoulders. Tumors that track me with their eyes. Should I put on a show? Demand this stranger respect my wife?

I contemplate indignation, but I realize I care more about what the stranger thinks than I do the subject of topic itself. "Why's that?" I ask.

"Look at this place. Where does it say *Dan?* Unless you haven't told me you like to collect bunny dolls and autographed photos of celebrities, I'd say this place is all Sylvia."

I swirl the eggs around on my plate. "I don't need much."

"Just a room in the basement."

"Something like that."

"Liar," she accuses. "Now be honest. When you saw me walk through the door, all inked up, what's the first thing that went through your mind? You must have had a pang of worry that you were getting some punk rocker chick that'd trash the place, didn't you?"

I took a sip from my coffee and leaned back against my chair. "Once, when I was younger—much younger—before Sylvia and Dylan, I almost took off just so I could go to New York and live a life of poverty and painting. All I wanted to do was tattoo the world with my art. The second I met you, I didn't see an ambitionless hooligan, a dope head, or a punk rocker. I saw a girl who appreciated art enough to use her body as a canvas."

She's quiet for a long time.

"I don't think you'd like Mark very much," she says.

"I'm sure Mark's great."

She shrugs. "He doesn't get me. If a wife has a master's in business, which I do, you'd think the husband might ask for help if the business the husband owned was losing money. You'd think. Not Mark. Male pride only goes so far, I've come to realize."

"Maybe you need to shoot straight with Mark," I say.

She grins at me. "Maybe I do."

She looks down at her plate, stabs a forkful of scrambled eggs and takes a bite. Her eyes close and she savors the taste. Her mouth is still full when she speaks. "These eggs are fantastic. They're so gooey." I can't lie to you: I felt a surge of male pride flash within me watching her lips wrap around my cooking.

"Thanks," I say. "Just add a lot of cheddar cheese."

We go on to talk about everything that sweeps through our minds. Coke vs. Pepsi, the perfect barbeque food, books, paintings, national parks, favorite movie quotes. Despite the ten-year age gap between us, we discover we have a lot in common. With every realization of our shared interests, the excitement that propelled our conversation cranked up a notch until we were nearly screaming at each other from across the table with giant smiles on our faces.

"...I love flip flops but I can't..."

"Dad."

"…drive a car with them on…"

"Dad!"

"…because the flip flops…"

"*Dad!*"

"…keep sticking to the floor!"

"Dad, I'm late for school!"

Suzanne and I lock eyes and immediately start laughing. Dylan looks from her to me, unaware of the joke. Maybe he just isn't used to seeing me smile.

"Come on, Dylan. Get your stuff. Dan, I'm sorry. Just leave all this. I'll clean it when I get back."

I'm still laughing. I look at my watch. I'm late for work, as well. But I don't care. The paint bucket would be waiting for me when I got there. I think that's a pretty good philosophy for life, if you ask me. Don't worry about the deadline or how many errands you can cram into a single afternoon after work. Just don't worry. The paint bucket will be waiting for you when you get there.

"Sounds good," I tell her.

She's helping put Dylan's backpack on his back. I enjoy watching him squirm and her struggle. "What do you have in here?" she asks him. "Rocks?" She turns to me. "Make sure you work up an appetite today. You're going to need it for tonight."

"I think I can manage that."

"I'm going to give you a meal so good, it'll make your head explode."

"Looking forward to it."

"Dylan, say good bye to your father."

"Bye, Dad."

"Bye, Dylan."

"Have a good day. Bye, Dan."

"Bye, Suzanne."

As I watch them leave my house, I think of the first time I watched her walk through the door. Soon, too soon, she'd leave just as she'd just done, and she wouldn't come back. It'd be Sylvia who'd walk through the door.

Sylvia never liked my eggs very much.

6.

A few days later, I sneak home during my lunch break to get a fresh T-shirt from the bedroom. It is brutally hot out, and I'd sweated through the one I was wearing. I make my way up the stairs to get another one from the bedroom when the bathroom door swings open. Suzanne pokes her head out from behind the door.

"Dan!" she says in a whisper. "Dan, come over here. Quick!"

I turn. "Suzanne?" I ask. I approached her. "Is everything all right?"

"Where's the nearest video guy?" she asks me. "Hurry!"

"Hank, I think. He's in the living room. Why?"

"Where's Larry?"

"I think he went to go to the van. I heard him say something about changing the battery."

Before I could blink, her hands shoot out and grab the front of my shirt. She jerks me inside and shuts the door behind me. She pushes me against the back of the door and leans in close.

"Look," she whispers. "I need to know. You're for real, right?"

"What?"

"I want to make this quick before Hank or Slelsnack find out we're up here. I just wanted to have a conversation with you, one that wasn't taped. I just need to know where I stand with you. Tell me. You're being you, right? You're not putting on any kind of act? Tell me you're not going to screw me over."

The bathroom is swirling with fog from the shower she'd just stepped from. Thick, watery heat filled the tiny room and for a moment, I feel like I was drowning.

"How could I do that?"

"I don't know! I didn't know what to expect when I showed up here. I don't watch a lot of reality TV, but some of the shows I've seen…I get weirded out how people can play a part, you know? Then I met you, and I thought to myself, 'Wow. This guy's being real.' I never should have come on this show. I don't know why I agreed to it. Mark only wanted more business for the parlor, but I'm starting to freak out here. This isn't me. I can't play a part. Always looking at that camera, wondering what it's recording, what people are going to think. But then I started to think that you felt the same way."

My shirt is still bunched in her fists, and I expect her to slam me against the door like a cop interrogating a perp. "*Tell* me I wasn't wrong. *Tell* everything we've talked about has been true. *Tell* me you've been you."

She is wearing a tight gray T-shirt. On the front stood a girl in oversized yellow rain boots holding an umbrella staring up at the storm that crashed down from above. I can't help but think of her as that girl, holding onto the smallest bit of hope under that umbrella while the dreams and promises she'd made for her life fell apart all around her.

I take her hands and gave her a reassuring squeeze. "I've been me, Suzanne," I say. "I'm not acting. Everything's real."

She breathes a relieved sigh and flattens her hands against my chest. For a moment, she rests her head against me. Her hair is still slightly wet from her shower, and I can smell the exotic fragrance of her shampoo. "Good," she says into my chest. "I thought so. I *hoped* so. I just needed to be sure."

Suddenly, she pushes her head away, grabs me by the shoulders and turns around. "Now, go. *Go!* I don't want them to catch us in here. They'll think we're up to something!"

She opens the door a crack and shoves me through. I turn around to get a good look at her just to make sure that the conversation had really happened, but she shut the door so quickly, I can't say whether or not it did.

When I look down, I see a wet patch on the front of my shirt, proving her existence like the Shroud of Turin.

7.

When I get back to work, I reach into my pocket to give Frank, one of the other painters, a five I owed him from the day before. I always keep my money in my pocket.

My fingers touch something unfamiliar.

A receipt?

I pull it out.

No, not a receipt.

A folded up piece of paper, the edge damp from the wet fingers that had placed it into my pocket. She would later tell me she'd written it the night before and had slipped it into my pocket when we were in the bathroom.

Dear Dan,

Is it possible that two strangers can find reality on a reality TV show? When I'm with you, it feels like I've just woken up after dreaming in a coma. I can't lie about this anymore. In these last few days, you've felt more like a husband to me than Mark ever did. I don't know what good this note will bring, if it brings any good at all. Am I crazy? Is it just the stress of the show and the glare of the lights or is it real? Is it really real?

That night when I get home, she stands beside the stove and bites her lip. She tries to pretend it's not on her mind. I'm afraid the cameras will catch something in our silence as we stare at one another, the space between us heavy with a shared secret.

After everything that happens later, I'm always asked, "How it felt when...?" For instance, "How did it feel when you read that note and answered her question?"

The best I can do is to compare it to a rollercoaster. You know that feeling when your cart slowly gets pulled up the hill? Your stomach gets lighter, and that butterfly flapping in your gut speeds up. And you know that moment right before your cart tips over, when it seems to pause a second before it hurtles downward? In that second you know you're doing something you shouldn't be doing. There's real danger that you could get hurt, but you don't care because you want to drop as fast as you can. For a second, you just want to fly. That's the closest I can get.

"It's really real," I tell her.

I've re-watched the footage I can't tell you how many times, and I can tell you in honesty that *this* is the moment.

This is the moment the cart tipped over the lip and sent me hurtling down the track.

What I didn't know then was that this rollercoaster ride would send me flying off the tracks completely.

8.

The next thing I know, it's Saturday. Suzanne leaves tomorrow. I tell her she's not cooking tonight. Tonight, we're going out. I haven't been able to talk to her about the note. To be fair, it added to the excitement, the danger. It felt like we were doing something wrong. It was a rush.

All I wanted was her. It was clear the moment I first laid eyes on her, but I couldn't hold it back from myself anymore. I didn't care about Sylvia's feelings. I did care about how I looked on TV, and I respected her wish to spare Mark from watching his wife cheat on him on television, but it didn't make it easier for me.

On that final Saturday, I take her and Dylan to The Rock Bottom. I feel a twinge of guilt for taking her *here* of all places (this is where Sylvia and I go when we go out), but it doesn't last long at all.

The Rock Bottom is the kind of place where you can get your run of the mill burger, if that's what you're feeling, or a pretty decent steak, if that's what you're feeling, too. It's not by any means fancy but fancy enough to make eating out feel special. Plus, the beer is cheap. Not the wine, though. Sylvia always orders the wine and always by the glass even though she kills nearly the entire bottle.

We enter—Suzanne, Dylan, Larry, Hank and Slelsnack—and I smell frying onions and the juicy sizzle of burgers on the grill.

Suzanne clasped her hands and closed her eyes. I want to kiss her. I fight the urge and don't let myself think about the fact that after tomorrow, I'll never see her again. After tomorrow, the girl of my dreams will fade, and the cold light of morning will shine on Sylvia instead.

Suzanne pulled on the rich, swirling scents from the grille. "I want whatever that is," she said. "I want *everything*. I'm so hungry."

"One, you came to the right place," I tell her. "Two, I won't stop you from getting whatever you want. The bill's on Arnie here."

The tables were already waiting for us. The reservation had been made earlier in the day by Slelsnack who arrived just before we did to have the manager sign a piece of paper, a one similar to the one I had, the one that tells you you'll wind up on TV if exchange for a little thing; you might have heard of it, but you don't really use it. It's as useless as your appendix or tonsils and only gets in the way. Just a little thing called your soul is all.

I've gotten used to the looks from people as I walk by towing a cameraman. The looks are a mix of resentment and jealousy but rarely amusement, which strikes me as odd. They don't mind living vicariously through avatars like me who they then criticize, threaten, obsess over, and jeer but they're *put out* when the very same shows they watch interrupt their night out?

Thankfully, we're ushered off to a private area. Suzanne, Dylan, and I at one table. The three stooges at another.

During the meal, Slelsnack receives a phone call. I'm told it's his partner, another producer who is with the camera crew on Sylvia's half of the show. He gets up to take the call, leaving the two stooges behind. I take the opportunity to go to the bathroom.

As I'm washing my hands, the door bursts inward.

"Oops! Wrong bathroom!" Suzanne says.

But she doesn't turn around.

She lets the door swing shut behind her.

Arnie's on the phone.

The camera guys are watching my kid.

No cameras, I realize.

Someone accidentally dropped the leash. Don't be surprised when you see the dog take off across the field.

Instinct takes over.

She lifts up. Her eyes close. I lean down.

The kiss is electric. It's a lightning bolt in the dark sky, like the streak that shoots through her hair. Twelve years of a bad marriage, twelve years of repression and submission and seven days of puppy love and raging lust explode in between the subatomic spaces where the molecules of my mouth bounce off of hers. We swap particles, leaving a little of ourselves with the other just in case this is a fairy tale without a happy ending.

As I sit here, I can still taste the salt from her margarita.

She places a hand on my chest. I break the kiss. I touch her hair, her face. She looks at me with those big, upturned, playful eyes.

Neither of us speak at first. It would only ruin the moment. Besides, each of us know what the other is thinking. We spoke with our lips but not in words. It's crazy, it's wrong, but it's too damn right to not try and make it work.

Eventually, I say, "What if I had been in the can?"

Then we both begin to laugh.

We laugh so hard we cry.

But we're not crying because we're laughing.

9.

When we get back, I notice a second production truck parked outside. I don't give it a second thought. Maybe I should have, but my head's still swimming from the kiss and what to do next. I need to know. The only thing I want to do is talk to her and figure this out.

Suzanne's quiet. The entire ride home she stared out the window. But she held my hand.

Even though Hank was in the back seat next to Dylan, rolling, she still held my hand. There was no turning back now.

She heads for the house as soon as I park the car. I don't wait for Hank or Dylan. I follow her in.

She heads up the stairs.

I follow.

She leads me to the bedroom. Downstairs I hear a car door slam. And another. I hear the pull of a van door.

I close the bedroom door behind me. She sits on the bed, head down.

"What do you want to do?" I ask her. "I know what I want, but it's only because I've been married longer. It's not going to work out with Sylvia and me. I don't know. Maybe you and Mark have a chance."

I sit down next to her. I can't stop the thrill that comes from sitting on my bed with her. I want to lean her back. I want to look at her hair spread across my bed. I want to kiss her again. I want to do a lot of things. I touch her knee. She rests her hand on top of mine.

"I want you to stay," I tell her. "I know this must be confusing, but it feels *right*. For the first time in my life, it just feels *right*."

I hear footsteps on the stairs. We don't have much time.

Suzanne looks at me with her beautiful, shining eyes. She's crying.

"I'm sorry, Dan," she says. "I'm so sorry."

The door bursts inward and a curtain of light blinds me. I wince, shield my eyes and try to get a good look.

I can't see well but I know *she's* there.

Sylvia.

"I *knew* it!" she shrieks.

I jump to my feet.

"Sylvia…you're not supposed to be back until…"

She flew at me and began to pound my head and shoulders. "I knew it! I knew it!" she screamed. I try to grab her hands but the camera lights are dizzying.

Why is Sylvia here?

Suzanne? Where is she going?

And then someone enters the room.

He steps in front of the camera lights while Suzanne slips behind him, and I get a good glimpse of him. I recognize him at once.

"Dan Grummet!" he says. "I'm Bobby Lodge, host of *Adulterers*. You've just been *caught!*"

The cameras sweep into the room.

Adulterers…I'm not on *Adulterers*, I want to tell him. You've got the wrong show. This is…

Wait, where's Suzanne?

The cameras…can't see…Suzanne…I don't understand…Sylvia's not supposed to be back…

"You're an asshole!" screams my wife. She blasts me good across the face. "You're a cheating asshole! No good! Lousy! *Loser!*"

The cameras move in close. The lights…can't see through the lights…Can't think, think, what's happening?

I get up. Sylvia's shrieking. I can't hear. Can't hear. Suzanne. The cameras stay on me. Adulterers? Suzanne saying, "I'm sorry, Dan. I'm so sorry."

"It wasn't real," I whisper. Amid the chaos of the moment, the microphone picks it up perfectly. It's an ominous moment of film. "None of it. None of it was real."

Her looking at my paintings, the cooking, the honesty, the note, flirting, the restaurant, the kiss…it was all an act for a TV show I didn't know I was on.

All this time, it was just a TV show.

My life ruined…for a TV show.

Sylvia. She set me up. Gave me hope for a better life. Ripped it away. Just so she could film it. Just so her tears could sparkle for America to see. She *ruined* me just so *she* could be famous.

Congratulations, Sylvia. I made you the most famous woman in America. I hope there are cameras for you in hell.

I don't think. The light is too bright to think.

The cameras follow me as I make my way to the closet. Sylvia continues to call me an asshole. Why can't she just shut up?

I open the closet door.

Reach for the top shelf.

I fired the gun before the box had time to fall to the floor. One of the cameras fell, continued to roll footage of the ceiling.

It was loud, *real* loud. The world cracked in half below us, and in that pit, I fell. I still fall. It didn't feel real. It never does, I guess or else no one would do it.

Sylvia screamed and tried to run, but Lodge and Larry clawed at each other in an effort to get out first.

I fired and fired again.

Lodge's head opened like a watermelon.

The back of Larry's throat exploded. He tried to scream but all that came out was a sputtering whistle through a smoking neck. He grabbed for his throat and fell to the floor, his mouth gaping like a fish on the deck of the boat.

Sylvia turned to me, her mouth open in fear and disbelief. She turned to flee. That's when I shot her. She crashed into the bureau; her arms flailed out and swept silver rings to the floor. Her final seconds of her life looked like she'd made a mad dash to the jewelry box to find the right accessory to bring into the next life.

Downstairs, I see Slelsnack in the center of the living room. He's stuck in place, unsure if what he heard from upstairs was what he *thought* he heard.

There's one last cameraman standing next to him, rolling footage.

I look at Slelsnack.

I think of his Hollywood smile. "Tears equal ratings," I say to him. He throws his hands up. A splash of brain and blood splatter the wall where my pictures were never allowed to hang. His body remains standing for a moment before collapsing a in a lifeless heap.

I hear a noise from the kitchen and whirl around.

Dylan stands in the doorway, his PSP at his feet. His mouth wide open looking at the blood-splattered man who used to be his father.

That's when I pass out.

11.

By now, you've all seen the footage. How could you have not? The first time the episode aired, it pulled in more viewers than the last episode of *M*A*S*H*, *Seinfeld,* and *The Tonight Show* with Johnny Carson.

It's pretty funny, in a way. I paint houses in suburbia, and I'm a better draw than Alan Alda, Jerry, and Johnny combined.

The footage was the most viewed video on *YouTube* and ran nonstop for about two months on *Entertainment Tonight, E! Entertainment Television, MSNBC,* and *Fox News.* In an effort to prolong the incident in a way that made me feel like they were fattening up a pig just so they would have more to eat, they interviewed everyone that ever knew me, even the guy that worked down at the local DB Mart where I bought my coffee every morning.

As for Suzanne? She was an actress, hired to play a part. She had left the bedroom by the time the shooting began and ran out of the house as soon as she heard the first shot. For a few months, *The Suzanne* was the most popular hair cut in America. If you guessed dyed-black hair with that funny little lightning bolt through it, come up and collect your prize. In the many interviews she conducted since that night, she says she never meant to hurt me but never had any real feelings for me. People have asked me if I regret not getting her, too. Of course not. She was just doing her job. It wasn't her fault. But I still get a kick how the media labeled her Jezebel. In the ensuing whirlwind, public opinion split down the middle. Half the country seemed to excuse what I did, saying it wasn't my fault, while the other half said I should have shot myself first and saved the bloodshed.

I don't disagree.

In retrospect, I should have read the fine print. My lawyers autopsied the contract I had signed. Nowhere does it say *Spouse Swap.* It's blatantly a contract for *Adulterers.* I was just too careless to notice.

It didn't stop me from suing the pants off of them.

Hundreds of other jilted husbands and wives joined me in the suit, claiming they had been set up, thinking they had signed on for a different show. Other actresses and actors like Suzanne came forward and admitted to the heist. The media ate this up. Just another scrap I threw to them. Were they surprised? Were they surprised that reality TV wasn't real at all?

As for me?

Don't feel bad for me.

Even in prison, I've got something that you don't. About a month ago, another fat, greasy producer approached me. His name's not Slelsnack, but I swear he hatched from the same nest of eggs as Arnie, and he wants me to star in a show about celebrities in prison. I think my response unnerved him because instead of answering him, I began to laugh. And I found that I couldn't stop. I just sat there behind the glass and laughed and laughed. Until I cried. It was the first time I cried since that night.

And somewhere I hope you're watching me, Sylvia.

Look at me now, Sylvia.

I'm a star.

XOXOX XOXOX XOXOX X

ABOUT THE AUTHOR

When he's not writing stories, Cooper O'Connor hunts for lake monsters in his kayak.

AUTHORS WANTED FOR

INK STAINS ANTHOLOGIES

We are looking for unique dark fiction submissions for upcoming editions of *Ink Stains Anthology* from Dark Alley Press.

Submissions are now open for pieces 3,000-20,0000 words for all works that fit under the Dark Alley Press banner, including those in the following categories:

- Dark fiction (including lit fic)
- Gothic fiction
- Supernatural/paranormal fiction
- Horror
- Steampunk
- Black Comedy
- Fantasy and Sci Fi

Authors of acquired pieces for Ink Stains Anthology will receive a flat fee payment upon publication. For more information, check out our website.

www.inkstainsanthology.com